THE DAILY SHER

THE DAILY

SHERLOCK HOLMES

A YEAR OF

QUOTES

FROM THE CASE-BOOK OF
THE WORLD'S GREATEST DETECTIVE

ARTHUR CONAN DOYLE

Edited by Levi Stahl and Stacey Shintani
With a Foreword by Michael Sims

The University of Chicago Press ✳ *Chicago and London*

The University of Chicago Press, Chicago 60637
The University of Chicago Press, Ltd., London
© 2019 by The University of Chicago
Foreword © 2019 by Michael Sims
Published 2019
Printed in the United States of America

28 27 26 25 24 23 22 21 20 19   1 2 3 4 5

ISBN-13: 978-0-226-65964-0 (paper)
ISBN-13: 978-0-226-65978-7 (e-book)
DOI: https://doi.org/10.7208/chicago/9780226659787.001.0001

Library of Congress Cataloging-in-Publication Data
Names: Doyle, Arthur Conan, 1859–1930, author. | Stahl, Levi,
    editor. | Shintani, Stacey, editor.
Title: The daily Sherlock Holmes : a year of quotes from the
    case-book of the world's greatest detective / Sir Arthur
    Conan Doyle ; edited by Levi Stahl and Stacey Shintani ;
    foreword by Michael Sims.
Description: Chicago ; London : The University of Chicago
    Press, 2019. | Includes index.
Identifiers: LCCN 2019015606 | ISBN 9780226659640 (pbk. : alk.
    paper) | ISBN 9780226659787 (e-book)
Subjects: LCSH: Holmes, Sherlock—Quotations.
Classification: LCC PR4621 .S73 2019 | DDC 823/.8—dc23
LC record available at https://lccn.loc.gov/2019015606

Foreword

A Dun-Coloured Veil Hung over the House-Tops

The tall bookcase just inside the door of my apartment holds books from my childhood and teen years: my earliest friends, still standing together as if posing for a class photo. Here are the primordial volumes I held while watching *Disney's Wonderful World of Color* in black and white in the 1960s. Here squat my halfling Big Little Books, with a picture facing every page of text in epics such as *Lassie: Adventure in Alaska*, wherein an earthquake coughs up a frozen mammoth.

Soon a detective-story theme appears. Encyclopedia Brown rakes in quarters by locating harmonicas and identifying vandals in Idaville. A much-loved Hardy Boys volume, *The Hooded Hawk Mystery*, is now ragged as an urchin but still upright. Between Scholastic paperbacks there stands, like a fat academic in the wrong ballroom, a single textbook, *Outlooks through Literature*, which opens "Unit One: *The Short Story*" with "The Adventure of the Speckled Band." A colorful painted montage portrays a woman in stages of collapse. Opposite, "'It is fear, Mr. Holmes. It is terror,'" reads the pull quote, promising that "these words were enough to challenge the

Master Detective, Sherlock Holmes, to an immediate investigation, some rapid deductions, and a brilliant solution."

Perhaps you could have read this teaser at thirteen and turned instead to watch *The Waltons*; since you hold this book in your hands, however, I doubt it. I could not. I think this was my first encounter with Sherlock Holmes as a character in a book. This story was my wardrobe that opened into Narnia, the tornado that whirled me to Oz. Recalling his own childhood, Arthur Conan Doyle once wrote, in an essay titled "Juvenilia," "I do not think that life has any joy to offer so complete, so soul-filling as that which comes upon the imaginative lad, whose spare time is limited, but who is able to snuggle down into a corner with his book, knowing that the next hour is all his own." He would be pleased to know how many people snuggle down with his own books almost a century after his death. When I met Holmes, I was in a wheelchair, thanks to juvenile rheumatic arthritis. Four decades later, I am a walking testament to the medicinal virtues of escapist fiction.

Within the lively pages of *The Daily Sherlock Holmes*, Stacey Shintani and Levi Stahl evoke what Sherlockians call the Canon. Their snapshots of atmosphere and clips of dialogue and action resurrect my teenage affair with Sherlock Holmes like a box full of love letters. They even cluster quotations into enlightening themes—Holmes's amusing rivalry with his older brother Mycroft, his fondness for the violin. They celebrate the chase, Holmes's sly technique of interrogating not only witnesses but also other detectives, his skepticism of authority. From January 1 on, Holmes's character is revealed— and, after all, it is this man's remarkable psyche that draws us into his cases.

I enjoy the musical rhythms of Victorian prose, but most of all I love the dialogue. The contrast between twenty-first-century American English and nineteenth-century British English wakes my own language for me. When asked what to do during a stakeout, Holmes replies, "Possess our souls in patience and make as little noise as possible." For a dangerous outing Holmes recommends a revolver and a toothbrush. "Depend upon it," he murmurs elsewhere, "there is nothing so unnatural as the commonplace." *The Daily Sherlock Holmes* includes many delicious mouthfuls of this dialect, such as Holmes's statement, "It is my belief, Watson, founded upon my experience, that the lowest and vilest alleys in London do not present a more dreadful record of sin than does the smiling and beautiful countryside."

Most charming of all is the ongoing conversation between Holmes and Watson. "I say, Watson," begins Holmes, and we perk up. The detective and the doctor are passionate talkers and great listeners. They don't just hold forth; they respond to each other. Doyle, a master of sketching character through dialogue, uses these conversations less to convey the details of his airy plots than to watch his team play together in a comedy of manners. After all but reading Watson's mind at Baker Street, Holmes remarks,

"The features are given to man as the means by which he shall express his emotions, and yours are faithful servants."

Elsewhere, "Have you the effrontery necessary to put it through?" Holmes asks Watson about a plan he has proposed.

"We can but try."

"Excellent, Watson! Compound of the Busy Bee and Excelsior. We can but try—the motto of the firm."

Despite Watson's marriage to Holmes's client Mary Morstan early in the series, this iconic team remains congenially yoked together over the years. Watson is always ready to assist our hero, and Holmes not only admits that he needs his Boswell but apologizes when he takes him for granted. People familiar only with cinematic impostures of Watson imagine that he is a loyal dunce, but the editors of this collection emphasize not only Watson's pluck but also his perceptive appraisal of Holmes's foibles and vanity.

This volume samples all of Doyle's narrative talents, which were not limited to dialogue. His chase scenes are legendary. He could also compose a nice cello overture of doom: "It was nine o'clock at night upon the second of August—the most terrible August in the history of the world. One might have thought already that God's curse hung heavy over a degenerate world, for there was an awesome hush and a feeling of vague expectancy in the sultry and stagnant air."

You will find your own favorites in *The Daily Sherlock Holmes*, but for me the *feel* of Sherlockian England is pressed like autumn leaves within its pages. Ever since I first began accompanying Holmes and Watson, I have loved the atmosphere, both literary and meteorological: "It was a foggy, cloudy morning, and a dun-coloured veil hung over the housetops, looking like the reflection of the mud-coloured streets beneath." I have felt a frisson of anticipation every time Watson or Holmes entered a hansom cab and "rattled through the crowded London streets." My own experiences of London streets have not dimmed this nostalgic romance, nor has my awareness of the dangers that Victorian smog created for lungs and purse. It doesn't matter that Holmes's original habitat has vanished from the real world. That's why we have literature, the great time machine.

Like Arthur Conan Doyle and Sherlock Holmes, Shintani and Stahl occasionally play games with their audience. The following pages include, for example, a spurious quotation solemnly attributed to a nonexistent Holmes story—but one that fans wish Doyle had written. This playfulness is in the spirit of the Baker Street Irregulars, the international organization that honors Holmes with banquets and toasts and lighthearted scholarship. I predict that you will dog-ear this volume, carry it in your pocket, read aloud from it.

Born among the wynds and closes of blustery Edinburgh in 1859, Doyle grew up reading writers such as Edgar Allan Poe. That outré American wrote a handful of detective stories, three of which featured a strutting French amateur named C. Auguste Dupin. Poe told readers that Dupin was a genius at observation, but he provided little evidence.

In 1886, after years of publishing minor stories anonymously, as was then the custom, the twenty-seven-year-old Arthur Conan Doyle, a fledgling MD, had an urge to write a detective story. He thought back a decade to his favorite professor in medical school at the University of Edinburgh, a renowned diagnostician named Joseph Bell. The good doctor inspired a brilliant detective because he was himself remarkably observant. Unlike Poe in his portrayal of Dupin, Doyle could provide countless examples of his hero's brilliance, because he had witnessed the method in medical school, day after day. Doyle was not the only student of Bell to record interactions such as the following (related in his article "The Truth about Sherlock Holmes"), in which his professor discerned a patient's history from a glance at his posture, clothing, and tan:

"Well, my man, you've served in the army?"

"Aye, sir."

"Not long discharged?"

"No, sir."

"A Highland regiment?"

"Aye, sir."

"A noncom officer?"

"Aye, sir."

Bell would explain his observations and inferences, and the devoted young Doyle would scribble copious notes.

Isn't literature a fine mystery? In the late 1880s and early 1890s, Doyle spends his off-hours dipping a pen in an ink bottle and writing his fine, neat hand across page after page. He rolls the stories up into mailing tubes and sends them out like messages in bottles. In a movie montage of rolling presses, publishers print the stories, and they shower down upon a public that does not yet know it suffers from a lack of heroes. Soon comes the day when Doyle casually writes to his mother, "Sherlock Holmes appears to have caught on."

In 1973, a couple of years after reading "The Speckled Band" in *Outlooks through Literature*, I received the two giant volumes of William S. Baring-Gould's *The Annotated Sherlock Holmes* from a mail-order book club called the Mystery Guild. They contained the species of footnotes and sidebars found in *Outlooks through Literature*, wherein I had learned about dogcarts and dark lanterns, but these glosses opened up to a tropical profusion of research and speculation: illustrations of hansom cabs, meditations on the supervillain snake of "The Speckled Band," biographies of illustrators. I stayed up all night.

Nowadays, when I prowl the bookshelves that hold my childhood and teenage treasures, I find myself reading Sherlock Holmes stories in the same mood in which I read natural history and science books. Holmes pays such close attention to the real world that he reminds us of cause and effect in this messy society, of the ripples that extend outward from our actions. I still admire Holmes's insights:

all those deductions from racing forms sticking out of coat pockets, inferences from a cabman's boots, cigar ash, and Watson's occasionally uneven shaving—Holmes following bicycle tire tracks in search of a kidnapped boy, or lying on the ground to peer with a scientist's eye at the grass we crush beneath our feet—

Often, on a cold, dark night, I wearily climb up the seventeen steps at 221B Baker Street and settle down with Holmes and Watson for the evening amid a cloud of pipe smoke. Mrs. Hudson has built a roaring fire. It glows like the light of reason to guard us from dangers that lurk out there in the fog.

Michael Sims

Preface

In making our selection of quotations for *The Daily Sherlock Holmes*, we aimed for a satisfying mix of variety, familiarity, comedy, action, dialogue, and description. We wanted longtime fans to feel welcomed back to cases and characters they love while also encountering forgotten gems from throughout the canon.

Attentive readers—and what other kind would Sherlock Holmes want?—will notice, however, that there are no selections from the final nine stories, as those are the only ones that now remain in copyright. While Holmes may not have scrupled at flouting the law to serve a larger purpose, we felt bound. We favored an uncluttered reading experience over textual exactitude, and so have silently altered capitalization and added closing punctuation where necessary.

As all but one of the stories we drew from were written from John Watson's point of view, readers can trust that any first-person narration not within quotation marks is his. An unidentified solo speaker within quotation marks can be assumed to be Holmes, barring a few instances where clear evidence indicates otherwise; in dialogue his voice is distinctive enough we trust you'll recognize him.

Now, to paraphrase the world's greatest detective: You know our methods. Enjoy them.

Stacey Shintani and Levi Stahl

THE DAILY SHERLOCK HOLMES

JANUARY

"I know, my dear Watson, that you share my love of all that is bizarre and outside the conventions and humdrum routine of everyday life. You have shown your relish for it by the enthusiasm which has prompted you to chronicle, and, if you will excuse my saying so, somewhat to embellish so many of my own little adventures."

"The Red-Headed League" (1891)

JANUARY 1

A STUDY IN SCARLET (1887)

"Dr. Watson, Mr. Sherlock Holmes," said Stamford, introducing us.

"How are you?" he said cordially, gripping my hand with a strength for which I should hardly have given him credit. "You have been in Afghanistan, I perceive."

"How on earth did you know that?" I asked in astonishment.

"Never mind," said he, chuckling to himself.

JANUARY 2

"THE ADVENTURE OF THE ABBEY GRANGE" (1904)

It was on a bitterly cold night and frosty morning, towards the end of the winter of '97, that I was awakened by a tugging at my shoulder. It was Holmes. The candle in his hand shone upon his eager, stooping face, and told me at a glance that something was amiss.

"Come, Watson, come!" he cried. "The game is afoot. Not a word! Into your clothes and come!"

"My mind," he said, "rebels at stagnation. Give me problems, give me work, give me the most abstruse cryptogram, or the most intricate analysis, and I am in my own proper atmosphere. I can dispense then with artificial stimulants. But I abhor the dull routine of existence. I crave for mental exaltation. That is why I have chosen my own particular profession, or rather created it, for I am the only one in the world."

"The only unofficial detective?" I said, raising my eyebrows.

"The only unofficial consulting detective," he answered. "I am the last and highest court of appeal in detection."

"On the fourth day after the New Year I heard my father give a sharp cry of surprise as we sat together at the breakfast table. There he was, sitting with a newly opened envelope in one hand and five dried orange pips in the outstretched palm of the other one." (—John Openshaw)

When I look at the three massive manuscript volumes which contain our work for the year 1894, I confess that it is very difficult for me, out of such a wealth of material, to select the cases which are most interesting in themselves, and at the same time most conducive to a display of those peculiar powers for which my friend was famous. As I turn over the pages, I see my notes upon the repulsive story of the red leech and the terrible death of Crosby, the banker. Here also I find an account of the Addleton tragedy, and the singular contents of the ancient British barrow. The famous Smith-Mortimer succession case comes also within this period, and so does the tracking and arrest of Huret, the Boulevard assassin—an exploit which won for Holmes an autograph letter of thanks from the French President and the Order of the Legion of Honour.

JANUARY 6

A STUDY IN SCARLET (1887)

His very person and appearance were such as to strike the attention of the most casual observer. In height he was rather over six feet, and so excessively lean that he seemed to be considerably taller.

His eyes were sharp and piercing, save during those intervals of torpor to which I have alluded; and his thin, hawk-like nose gave his whole expression an air of alertness and decision. His chin, too, had the prominence and squareness which mark the man of determination. His hands were invariably blotted with ink and stained with chemicals, yet he was possessed of extraordinary delicacy of touch, as I frequently had occasion to observe when I watched him manipulating his fragile philosophical instruments.

JANUARY 7

"THE ADVENTURE OF THE BERYL CORONET" (1892)

"It is an old maxim of mine that when you have excluded the impossible, whatever remains, however improbable, must be the truth."

JANUARY 8

"THE ADVENTURE OF THE BLUE CARBUNCLE" (1892)

I seated myself in his armchair and warmed my hands before his crackling fire, for a sharp frost had set in, and the windows were thick with the ice crystals. "I suppose," I remarked, "that, homely as it looks, this [hat] has some deadly story linked on to it—that it is the clue which will guide you in the solution of some mystery, and the punishment of some crime."

"No, no. No crime," said Sherlock Holmes, laughing. "Only one of those whimsical little incidents which will happen when you have four million human beings all jostling each other within the space of a few square miles. Amid the action and reaction of so dense a swarm of humanity, every possible combination of events may be expected to take place, and many a little problem will be presented which may be striking and bizarre without being criminal."

JANUARY 9

"THE ADVENTURE OF THE DANCING MEN" (1903)

"Perhaps you can account also for the bullet which has so obviously struck the edge of the window?"

He had turned suddenly, and his long, thin finger was pointing to a hole which had been drilled right through the lower window-sash, about an inch above the bottom.

"By George!" cried the inspector. "How ever did you see that?"

"Because I looked for it."

JANUARY 10

"By the way, Holmes," I added, "I have no doubt the connection between my boots and a Turkish bath is a perfectly self-evident one to a logical mind, and yet I should be obliged to you if you would indicate it."

"The train of reasoning is not very obscure, Watson," said Holmes with a mischievous twinkle. "It belongs to the same elementary class of deduction which I should illustrate if I were to ask you who shared your cab in your drive this morning."

JANUARY 11

"An old soldier, I perceive," said Sherlock.

"And very recently discharged," remarked the brother.

"Served in India, I see."

"And a non-commissioned officer."

"Royal Artillery, I fancy," said Sherlock.

"And a widower."

"But with a child."

"Children, my dear boy, children."

"Come," said I, laughing, "this is a little too much."

"If I remember rightly, you on one occasion, in the early days of our friendship, defined my limits in a very precise fashion."

"Yes," I answered, laughing. "It was a singular document. Philosophy, astronomy, and politics were marked at zero, I remember. Botany variable, geology profound as regards the mud stains from any region within fifty miles of town, chemistry eccentric, anatomy unsystematic, sensational literature and crime records unique, violin player, boxer, swordsman, lawyer, and self-poisoner by cocaine and tobacco. Those, I think, were the main points of my analysis."

"Do you see any clue?"

"You have furnished me with seven, but of course I must test them before I can pronounce upon their value."

"You suspect someone?"

"I suspect myself."

"What!"

"Of coming to conclusions too rapidly."

JANUARY 14

In recording from time to time some of the curious experiences and interesting recollections which I associate with my long and intimate friendship with Mr. Sherlock Holmes, I have continually been faced by difficulties caused by his own aversion to publicity. To his sombre and cynical spirit all popular applause was always abhorrent, and nothing amused him more at the end of a successful case than to hand over the actual exposure to some orthodox official, and to listen with a mocking smile to the general chorus of misplaced congratulation.

JANUARY 15

"Written in pencil upon the fly-leaf of a book, octavo size, no water-mark. Hum! Posted to-day at Gravesend by a man with a dirty thumb. Ha! And the flap has been gummed, if I am not very much in error, by a person who had been chewing tobacco."

JANUARY 16

A STUDY IN SCARLET (1887)

"They say that genius is an infinite capacity for taking pains," he remarked with a smile. "It's a very bad definition, but it does apply to detective work."

JANUARY 17

"THE RED-HEADED LEAGUE" (1891)

I took a good look at the man and endeavoured, after the fashion of my companion, to read the indications which might be presented by his dress or appearance.

I did not gain very much, however, by my inspection. Our visitor bore every mark of being an average commonplace British tradesman, obese, pompous, and slow. He wore rather baggy grey shepherd's check trousers, a not over-clean black frock-coat, unbuttoned in the front, and a drab waistcoat with a heavy brassy Albert chain, and a square pierced bit of metal dangling down as an ornament. A frayed top-hat and a faded brown overcoat with a wrinkled velvet collar lay upon a chair beside him. Altogether, look as I would, there was nothing remarkable about the man save his blazing red head, and the expression of extreme chagrin and discontent upon his features.

Sherlock Holmes's quick eye took in my occupation, and he shook his head with a smile as he noticed my questioning glances. "Beyond the obvious facts that he has at some time done manual labour, that he takes snuff, that he is a Freemason, that he has been in China, and that he has done a considerable amount of writing lately, I can deduce nothing else."

JANUARY 18

"SILVER BLAZE" (1892)

"Nothing clears up a case so much as stating it to another person."

JANUARY 19

THE HOUND OF THE BASKERVILLES (1902)

"Well, Watson, what do you make of it?"

Holmes was sitting with his back to me, and I had given him no sign of my occupation.

"How did you know what I was doing? I believe you have eyes in the back of your head."

"I have, at least, a well-polished, silver-plated coffee-pot in front of me."

THE SIGN OF FOUR (1890)

"There is nothing more unaesthetic than a police-man."

"THE ADVENTURE OF THE ABBEY GRANGE" (1904)

"I must admit, Watson, that you have some power of selection, which atones for much which I deplore in your narratives. Your fatal habit of looking at everything from the point of view of a story instead of as a scientific exercise has ruined what might have been an instructive and even classical series of demonstrations. You slur over work of the utmost finesse and delicacy, in order to dwell upon sensational details which may excite, but cannot possibly instruct, the reader."

"Why do you not write them yourself?" I said, with some bitterness.

"I will, my dear Watson, I will. At present I am, as you know, fairly busy, but I propose to devote my declining years to the composition of a text-book, which shall focus the whole art of detection into one volume."

JANUARY 22

"I think there are certain crimes which the law cannot touch, and which therefore, to some extent, justify private revenge."

JANUARY 23

"Good-evening, Doctor [Trevelyan]," said Holmes cheerily. "I am glad to see that you have only been waiting a very few minutes."

"You spoke to my coachman, then?"

"No, it was the candle on the side-table that told me."

JANUARY 24

"Ha!" cried Gregson, in a relieved voice; "you should never neglect a chance, however small it may seem."

"To a great mind, nothing is little," remarked Holmes, sententiously.

JANUARY 25

"I found the ash of a cigar, which my special knowledge of tobacco ashes enabled me to pronounce as an Indian cigar. I have, as you know, devoted some attention to this, and written a little monograph on the ashes of 140 different varieties of pipe, cigar, and cigarette tobacco."

JANUARY 26

"I think of writing another little monograph some of these days on the typewriter and its relation to crime. It is a subject to which I have devoted some little attention."

JANUARY 27

"I am fairly familiar with all forms of secret writings, and am myself the author of a trifling monograph upon the subject, in which I analyze one hundred and sixty separate ciphers."

JANUARY 28

"I have serious thoughts of writing a small monograph upon the uses of dogs in the work of the detective."

JANUARY 29

One of the most remarkable characteristics of Sherlock Holmes was his power of throwing his brain out of action and switching all thoughts on to lighter things whenever he had convinced himself that he could no longer work to advantage. I remember that during the whole of that memorable day he lost himself in a monograph which he had undertaken upon the Polyphonic Motets of Lassus.

JANUARY 30

"But your appearance, Holmes—your ghastly face?"

"Three days of absolute fast does not improve one's beauty, Watson. For the rest, there is nothing which a sponge may not cure. With vaseline upon one's forehead, belladonna in one's eyes, rouge over the cheek-bones, and crusts of beeswax round one's lips, a very satisfying effect can be produced. Malingering is a subject upon which I have sometimes thought of writing a monograph. A little occasional talk about half-crowns, oysters, or any other extraneous subject produces a pleasing effect of delirium."

JANUARY 31

"THE RED-HEADED LEAGUE" (1891)

"You reasoned it out beautifully," I exclaimed, in unfeigned admiration. "It is so long a chain, and yet every link rings true."

"It saved me from ennui," he answered, yawning. "Alas! I already feel it closing in upon me. My life is spent in one long effort to escape from the commonplaces of existence. These little problems help me to do so."

FEBRUARY

When we returned to Mrs. Warren's rooms, the gloom of a London winter evening had thickened into one grey curtain, a dead monotone of colour, broken only by the sharp yellow squares of the windows and the blurred haloes of the gas-lamps. As we peered from the darkened sitting-room of the lodging-house, one more dim light glimmered high up through the obscurity.

"Someone is moving in that room," said Holmes in a whisper, his gaunt and eager face thrust forward to the window-pane. "Yes, I can see his shadow. There he is again!"

"The Adventure of the Red Circle" (1911)

Looking over his shoulder, I saw that on the pavement opposite there stood a large woman with a heavy fur boa round her neck, and a large curling red feather in a broad-brimmed hat which was tilted in a coquettish Duchess-of-Devonshire fashion over her ear. From under this great panoply she peeped up in a nervous, hesitating fashion at our windows, while her body oscillated backwards and forwards, and her fingers fidgeted with her glove buttons. Suddenly, with a plunge, as of the swimmer who leaves the bank, she hurried across the road, and we heard the sharp clang of the bell.

"I have seen those symptoms before," said Holmes, throwing his cigarette into the fire. "Oscillation upon the pavement always means an *affaire de coeur*. She would like advice, but is not sure that the matter is not too delicate for communication. And yet even here we may discriminate. When a woman has been seriously wronged by a man she no longer oscillates, and the usual symptom is a broken bell wire. Here we may take it that there is a love matter, but that the maiden is not so much angry as perplexed, or grieved. But here she comes in person to relieve our doubts."

FEBRUARY 2

Soames hesitated.

"It is a very delicate question," said he. "One hardly likes to throw suspicion where there are no proofs."

"Let us hear the suspicions. I will look after the proofs."

FEBRUARY 3

Sherlock Holmes closed his eyes and placed his elbows upon the arms of his chair, with his finger-tips together. "The ideal reasoner," he remarked, "would, when he has once been shown a single fact in all its bearings, deduce from it not only all the chain of events which led up to it but also all the results which would follow from it."

FEBRUARY 4

"By Jove!" I cried; "if he really wants someone to share the rooms and the expense, I am the very man for him. I should prefer having a partner to being alone."

Young Stamford looked rather strangely at me over his wineglass. "You don't know Sherlock Holmes yet," he said; "perhaps you would not care for him as a constant companion."

"Why, what is there against him?"

"Oh, I didn't say there was anything against him. He is a little queer in his ideas—an enthusiast in some branches of science. As far as I know he is a decent fellow enough."

FEBRUARY 5

THE SIGN OF FOUR (1890)

Standing at the window, I watched her walking briskly down the street until the grey turban and white feather were but a speck in the sombre crowd.

"What a very attractive woman!" I exclaimed, turning to my companion.

He had lit his pipe again and was leaning back with drooping eyelids. "Is she?" he said languidly; "I did not observe."

"You really are an automaton—a calculating machine," I cried. "There is something positively inhuman in you at times."

FEBRUARY 6

"But pray tell me, before we go farther, who it is that I have the pleasure of assisting."

The man hesitated for an instant. "My name is John Robinson," he answered with a sidelong glance.

"No, no; the real name," said Holmes, sweetly. "It is always awkward doing business with an alias."

FEBRUARY 7

As we drove up, we found the railings in front of the house lined by a curious crowd. Holmes whistled.

"By George! it's attempted murder at the least. Nothing less will hold the London message-boy. There's a deed of violence indicated in that fellow's round shoulders and outstretched neck."

FEBRUARY 8

Our route was certainly a singular one. Holmes's knowledge of the byways of London was extraordinary, and on this occasion he passed rapidly and with an assured step through a network of mews and stables, the very existence of which I had never known.

FEBRUARY 9

"THE DISAPPEARANCE OF LADY FRANCES CARFAX" (1911)

"Where is your warrant?"

Holmes half drew a revolver from his pocket. "This will have to serve till a better one comes."

"Why, you are a common burglar."

"So you might describe me," said Holmes cheerfully. "My companion is also a dangerous ruffian. And together we are going through your house."

FEBRUARY 10

"THE BOSCOMBE VALLEY MYSTERY" (1891)

"And the murderer?"

"Is a tall man, left-handed, limps with the right leg, wears thick-soled shooting boots and a grey cloak, smokes Indian cigars, uses a cigar-holder, and carries a blunt penknife in his pocket. There are several other indications, but these may be enough to aid us in our search."

FEBRUARY 11
"THE FIVE ORANGE PIPS" (1891)

"A man should keep his little brain-attic stocked with all the furniture that he is likely to use, and the rest he can put away in the lumber room of his library, where he can get it if he wants it."

FEBRUARY 12
"THE ADVENTURE OF THE BLUE CARBUNCLE" (1892)

"My name is Sherlock Holmes. It is my business to know what other people don't know."

FEBRUARY 13
"SILVER BLAZE" (1892)

"Why didn't you go down yesterday?"

"Because I made a blunder, my dear Watson—which is, I am afraid, a more common occurrence than anyone would think who only knew me through your memoirs."

Miss Morstan and I stood together, and her hand was in mine. A wondrous subtle thing is love, for here were we two, who had never seen each other before that day, between whom no word or even look of affection had ever passed, and yet now in an hour of trouble our hands instinctively sought for each other. I have marvelled at it since, but at the time it seemed the most natural thing that I should go out to her so, and, as she has often told me, there was in her also the instinct to turn to me for comfort and protection. So we stood hand in hand like two children, and there was peace in our hearts for all the dark things that surrounded us.

To Sherlock Holmes she is always *the* woman. I have seldom heard him mention her under any other name. In his eyes she eclipses and predominates the whole of her sex. It was not that he felt any emotion akin to love for Irene Adler. All emotions, and that one particularly, were abhorrent to his cold, precise but admirably balanced mind. He was, I take it, the most perfect reasoning and observing machine that the world has seen; but, as a lover, he would have placed himself in a false position. He never spoke of the softer passions, save with a gibe and a sneer. They were admirable things for the observer—excellent for drawing the veil from men's motives and actions. But for the trained reasoner to admit such intrusions into his own delicate and finely adjusted temperament was to introduce a distracting factor which might throw a doubt upon all his mental results. Grit in a sensitive instrument, or a crack in one of his own high-power lenses, would not be more disturbing than a strong emotion in a nature such as his. And yet there was but one woman to him, and that woman was the late Irene Adler, of dubious and questionable memory.

FEBRUARY 16

"THE ADVENTURE OF THE COPPER BEECHES" (1892)

"I have devised seven separate explanations, each of which would cover the facts as far as we know them."

FEBRUARY 17

"THE ADVENTURE OF THE RED CIRCLE" (1911)

"It opens a pleasing field for intelligent speculation. The words are written with a broad-pointed, violet-tinted pencil of a not unusual pattern. You will observe that the paper is torn away at the side here after the printing was done, so that the 'S' of 'SOAP' is partly gone. Suggestive, Watson, is it not?"

"Of caution?"

"Exactly."

FEBRUARY 18

"THE ADVENTURE OF THE DEVIL'S FOOT" (1910)

"Well, then, I take our powder—or what remains of it—from the envelope, and I lay it above the burning lamp. So! Now, Watson, let us sit down and await developments."

They were not long in coming. I had hardly settled in my chair before I was conscious of a thick, musky odour, subtle and nauseous. At the very first whiff of it my brain and my imagination were beyond all control. A thick, black cloud swirled before my eyes, and my mind told me that in this cloud, unseen as yet, but about to spring out upon my appalled senses, lurked all that was vaguely horrible, all that was monstrous and inconceivably wicked in the universe.

FEBRUARY 19

"THE ADVENTURE OF THE
MISSING THREE-QUARTER" (1904)

He chuckled and rubbed his hands when we found ourselves in the street once more.

"Well?" I asked.

"We progress, my dear Watson, we progress. I had seven different schemes for getting a glimpse of that telegram, but I could hardly hope to succeed the very first time."

FEBRUARY 20

"THE ADVENTURE OF BLACK PETER" (1904)

Holmes was working somewhere under one of the numerous disguises and names with which he concealed his own formidable identity. He had at least five small refuges in different parts of London, in which he was able to change his personality.

FEBRUARY 21

"THE ADVENTURE OF THE
MISSING THREE-QUARTER" (1904)

Holmes rose. Taking the [telegraph] forms, he carried them over to the window and carefully examined that which was uppermost.

"It is a pity he did not write in pencil," said he, throwing them down again with a shrug of disappointment. "As you have no doubt frequently observed, Watson, the impression usually goes through—a fact which has dissolved many a happy marriage."

FEBRUARY 22
"THE ADVENTURE OF THE DEVIL'S FOOT" (1910)

"Upon my word, Watson!" said Holmes at last with an unsteady voice, "I owe you both my thanks and an apology. It was an unjustifiable experiment even for one's self, and doubly so for a friend. I am really very sorry."

"You know," I answered with some emotion, for I had never seen so much of Holmes's heart before, "that it is my greatest joy and privilege to help you."

He relapsed at once into the half-humorous, half-cynical vein which was his habitual attitude to those about him.

FEBRUARY 23
"THE NAVAL TREATY" (1893)

"The authorities are excellent at amassing facts, though they do not always use them to advantage."

FEBRUARY 24
"THE REIGATE SQUIRES" (1893)

"It is of the highest importance in the art of detection to be able to recognize, out of a number of facts, which are incidental and which vital. Otherwise your energy and attention must be dissipated instead of being concentrated."

FEBRUARY 25
"THE MUSGRAVE RITUAL" (1893)

An anomaly which often struck me in the character of my friend Sherlock Holmes was that, although in his methods of thought he was the neatest and most methodical of mankind, and although also he affected a certain quiet primness of dress, he was none the less in his personal habits one of the most untidy men that ever drove a fellow-lodger to distraction.

FEBRUARY 26
"THE ADVENTURE OF THE DYING DETECTIVE" (1913)

Mrs. Hudson, the landlady of Sherlock Holmes, was a long-suffering woman. Not only was her first-floor flat invaded at all hours by throngs of singular and often undesirable characters but her remarkable lodger showed an eccentricity and irregularity in his life which must have sorely tried her patience. His incredible untidiness, his addiction to music at strange hours, his occasional revolver practice within doors, his weird and often malodorous scientific experiments, and the atmosphere of violence and danger which hung around him made him the very worst tenant in London. On the other hand, his payments were princely. I have no doubt that the house might have been purchased at the price which Holmes paid for his rooms during the years that I was with him.

FEBRUARY 27

A STUDY IN SCARLET (1887)

"It was easier to know it than to explain why I knew it. If you were asked to prove that two and two made four, you might find some difficulty, and yet you are quite sure of the fact."

FEBRUARY 28

"THE ADVENTURE OF THE SIX NAPOLEONS" (1904)

Lestrade and I sat silent for a moment, and then, with a spontaneous impulse, we both broke out clapping, as at the well-wrought crisis of a play. A flush of colour sprang to Holmes's pale cheeks, and he bowed to us like the master dramatist who receives the homage of his audience. It was at such moments that for an instant he ceased to be a reasoning machine, and betrayed his human love for admiration and applause. The same singularly proud and reserved nature which turned away with disdain from popular notoriety was capable of being moved to its depths by spontaneous wonder and praise from a friend.

FEBRUARY 29

THE EXTRAORDINARY ADVENTURES OF
ARSÈNE LUPIN, GENTLEMAN-BURGLAR (1910)

By Maurice Leblanc

Holmes smiled and said: "Monsieur Devanne, everybody cannot solve riddles."

MARCH

It was a cold, dark March evening, with a sharp wind and a fine rain beating upon our faces, a fit setting for the wild common over which our road passed and the tragic goal to which it led us.

"The Adventure of Wisteria Lodge" (1908)

In glancing over my notes of the seventy odd cases in which I have during the last eight years studied the methods of my friend Sherlock Holmes, I find many tragic, some comic, a large number merely strange, but none commonplace; for, working as he did rather for the love of his art than for the acquirement of wealth, he refused to associate himself with any investigation which did not tend towards the unusual, and even the fantastic.

"Was there any feature of interest?"

"I fancy not. The thieves ransacked the library and got very little for their pains. The whole place was turned upside down, drawers burst open, and presses ransacked, with the result that an odd volume of Pope's *Homer*, two plated candlesticks, an ivory letter-weight, a small oak barometer, and a ball of twine are all that have vanished."

"What an extraordinary assortment!" I exclaimed.

"Oh, the fellows evidently grabbed hold of everything they could get."

Holmes grunted from the sofa.

"The county police ought to make something of

that," said he; "why, it is surely obvious that—"

But I held up a warning finger.

"You are here for a rest, my dear fellow. For heaven's sake don't get started on a new problem when your nerves are all in shreds."

MARCH 3
"A CASE OF IDENTITY" (1891)

"You appeared to read a good deal upon her which was quite invisible to me," I remarked.

"Not invisible, but unnoticed, Watson. You did not know where to look, and so you missed all that was important. I can never bring you to realize the importance of sleeves, the suggestiveness of thumbnails, or the great issues that may hang from a bootlace."

MARCH 4
A STUDY IN SCARLET (1887)

"I never read such rubbish in my life."

"What is it?" asked Sherlock Holmes.

"Why, this article," I said, pointing at it with my egg spoon as I sat down to my breakfast. "I see that you have read it since you have marked it. I don't deny that it is smartly written. It irritates me though. It is evidently the theory of some armchair lounger who evolves all these neat little paradoxes in the seclusion of his own study. It is not practical. I should like to see him clapped down in a third class carriage on the Underground, and asked to give the trades of all his fellow-travellers. I would lay a thousand to one against him."

"You would lose your money," Sherlock Holmes remarked calmly. "As for the article, I wrote it myself."

MARCH 5

"THE ADVENTURE OF CHARLES AUGUSTUS
MILVERTON" (1904)

"Well, I don't like it, but I suppose it must be," said I. "When do we start?"

"You are not coming."

"Then you are not going," said I. "I give you my word of honour—and I never broke it in my life—that I will take a cab straight to the police-station and give you away, unless you let me share this adventure with you."

"You can't help me."

"How do you know that? You can't tell what may happen. Anyway, my resolution is taken. Other people besides you have self-respect, and even reputations."

MARCH 6

"Data! data! data!" he cried impatiently. "I can't make bricks without clay."

MARCH 7

It was a perfect day, with a bright sun and a few fleecy clouds in the heavens. The trees and wayside hedges were just throwing out their first green shoots, and the air was full of the pleasant smell of the moist earth. To me at least there was a strange contrast between the sweet promise of the spring and this sinister quest upon which we were engaged.

MARCH 8

"May I ask whether you have any professional inquiry on foot at present?"

"None. Hence the cocaine. I cannot live without brainwork. What else is there to live for? Stand at the window here. Was ever such a dreary, dismal, unprofitable world? See how the yellow fog swirls down the street and drifts across the dun-coloured houses. What could be more hopelessly prosaic and material? What is the use of having powers, Doctor, when one has no field upon which to exert them? Crime is commonplace, existence is commonplace, and no qualities save those which are commonplace have any function upon earth."

MARCH 9
A STUDY IN SCARLET (1887)

Desultory readers are seldom remarkable for the exactness of their learning. No man burdens his mind with small matters unless he has some very good reason for doing so.

MARCH 10
"A CASE OF IDENTITY" (1891)

"Do you not find," he said, "that with your short sight it is a little trying to do so much typewriting?"

"I did at first," she answered, "but now I know where the letters are without looking." Then, suddenly realizing the full purport of his words, she gave a violent start, and looked up with fear and astonishment upon her broad, good-humoured face. "You've heard about me, Mr. Holmes," she cried, "else how could you know all that?"

"Never mind," said Holmes, laughing; "it is my business to know things."

MARCH 11
"THE BOSCOMBE VALLEY MYSTERY" (1891)

"There is nothing more deceptive than an obvious fact."

MARCH 12
"THE GREEK INTERPRETER" (1893)

"There are many men in London, you know, who, some from shyness, some from misanthropy, have no wish for the company of their fellows. Yet they are not averse to comfortable chairs and the latest periodicals. It is for the convenience of these that the Diogenes Club was started, and it now contains the most unsociable and unclubbable men in town. No member is permitted to take the least notice of any other one. Save in the Stranger's Room, no talking is, under any circumstances, allowed, and three offenses, if brought to the notice of the committee, render the talker liable to expulsion. My brother was one of the founders, and I have myself found it a very soothing atmosphere."

MARCH 13

"And a singularly consistent investigation you have made, my dear Watson," said he. "I cannot at the moment recall any possible blunder which you have omitted. The total effect of your proceeding has been to give the alarm everywhere and yet to discover nothing."

MARCH 14

We had arrived before the doctor or the police, so that everything was absolutely undisturbed. Let me describe exactly the scene as we saw it upon that misty March morning. It has left an impression which can never be effaced from my mind.

MARCH 15

Holmes was accessible upon the side of flattery, and also, to do him justice, upon the side of kindliness.

MARCH 16

These were the two men who entered abruptly into our little sitting-room on Tuesday, March the 16th, shortly after our breakfast hour, as we were smoking together, preparatory to our daily excursion upon the moors.

"Mr. Holmes," said the vicar in an agitated voice, "the most extraordinary and tragic affair has occurred during the night. It is the most unheard-of business. We can only regard it as a special Providence that you should chance to be here at the time, for in all England you are the one man we need."

MARCH 17

"And this? Ha, ha! What have we here? Tip-toes! tip-toes! Square, too, quite unusual boots! They come, they go, they come again—of course that was for the cloak."

MARCH 18

He took down the great book in which, day by day, he filed the agony columns of the various London journals. "Dear me!" said he, turning over the pages, "what a chorus of groans, cries, and bleatings! What a rag-bag of singular happenings! But surely the most valuable hunting-ground that ever was given to a student of the unusual!"

MARCH 19
"THE ADVENTURE OF THE EMPTY HOUSE" (1903)

"Work is the best antidote to sorrow, my dear Watson."

MARCH 20
"A SCANDAL IN BOHEMIA" (1891)

One night—it was on the twentieth of March, 1888—I was returning from a journey to a patient (for I had now returned to civil practice), when my way led me through Baker Street. As I passed the well-remembered door, which must always be associated in my mind with my wooing, and with the dark incidents of the Study in Scarlet, I was seized with a keen desire to see Holmes again, and to know how he was employing his extraordinary powers. His rooms were brilliantly lit, and, even as I looked up, I saw his tall, spare figure pass twice in a dark silhouette against the blind. He was pacing the room swiftly, eagerly, with his head sunk upon his chest and his hands clasped behind him. To me, who knew his every mood and habit, his attitude and manner told their own story. He was at work again. He had risen out of his drug-created dreams and was hot upon the scent of some new problem.

MARCH 21

"THE ADVENTURE OF THE
MISSING THREE-QUARTER" (1904)

"We have only to find to whom that telegram is addressed," I suggested.

"Exactly, my dear Watson. Your reflection, though profound, had already crossed my mind."

MARCH 22

"THE RED-HEADED LEAGUE" (1891)

My friend was an enthusiastic musician, being himself not only a very capable performer but a composer of no ordinary merit. All the afternoon he sat in the stalls wrapped in the most perfect happiness, gently waving his long, thin fingers in time to the music, while his gently smiling face and his languid, dreamy eyes were as unlike those of Holmes, the sleuth-hound, Holmes the relentless, keen-witted, ready-handed criminal agent, as it was possible to conceive. In his singular character the dual nature alternately asserted itself, and his extreme exactness and astuteness represented, as I have often thought, the reaction against the poetic and contemplative mood which occasionally predominated in him. The swing of his nature took him from extreme languor to devouring energy; and, as I knew well, he was never so truly formidable as when, for days on end, he had been lounging in his armchair amid his improvisations and his black-letter editions. Then it was that the lust of the chase would suddenly come upon him, and that his brilliant reasoning power would rise to the level of intuition, until those who were unacquainted with his methods would look askance at him as on a man whose knowledge was not that of other mortals.

MARCH 23
"THE PROBLEM OF THOR BRIDGE" (1922)

"You've done yourself no good this morning, Mr. Holmes, for I have broken stronger men than you. No man ever crossed me and was the better for it."

"So many have said so, and yet here I am," said Holmes, smiling.

MARCH 24

A lean, ferret-like man, furtive and sly-looking, was waiting for us upon the platform. In spite of the light brown dustcoat and leather leggings which he wore in deference to his rustic surroundings, I had no difficulty in recognizing Lestrade, of Scotland Yard.

MARCH 25

"THE ADVENTURE OF THE DANCING MEN" (1903)

"What one man can invent another can discover."

MARCH 26

"THE ADVENTURE OF THE PRIORY SCHOOL" (1904)

"Well, well," said he, at last. "It is, of course, possible that a cunning man might change the tyres of his bicycle in order to leave unfamiliar tracks. A criminal who was capable of such a thought is a man whom I should be proud to do business with."

MARCH 27

I find it recorded in my notebook that it was a bleak and windy day towards the end of March in the year 1892. Holmes had received a telegram while we sat at our lunch, and he had scribbled a reply. He made no remark, but the matter remained in his thoughts, for he stood in front of the fire afterwards with a thoughtful face, smoking his pipe, and casting an occasional glance at the message. Suddenly he turned upon me with a mischievous twinkle in his eyes.

MARCH 28

All that day and the next and the next Holmes was in a mood which his friends would call taciturn, and others morose. He ran out and ran in, smoked incessantly, played snatches on his violin, sank into reveries, devoured sandwiches at irregular hours, and hardly answered the casual questions which I put to him. It was evident to me that things were not going well with him or his quest.

MARCH 29

"I'm a busy man and I can't waste time. I'm going into that bedroom. Pray make yourselves quite at home in my absence. You can explain to your friend how the matter lies without the restraint of my presence. I shall try over the Hoffmann 'Barcarole' upon my violin. In five minutes I shall return for your final answer. You quite grasp the alternative, do you not?"

MARCH 30

"There is nothing more to be said or to be done tonight, so hand me over my violin and let us try to forget for half an hour the miserable weather, and the still more miserable ways of our fellow men."

MARCH 31

"And now, Doctor, we've done our work, so it's time we had some play. A sandwich and a cup of coffee, and then off to violin-land, where all is sweetness and delicacy and harmony, and there are no redheaded clients to vex us with their conundrums."

APRIL

It was an ideal spring day, a light blue sky, flecked with little fleecy white clouds drifting across from west to east. The sun was shining very brightly, and yet there was an exhilarating nip in the air, which set an edge to a man's energy. All over the countryside, away to the rolling hills around Aldershot, the little red and grey roofs of the farm-steadings peeped out from amid the light green of the new foliage.

"Are they not fresh and beautiful?" I cried with all the enthusiasm of a man fresh from the fogs of Baker Street.

But Holmes shook his head gravely.

"Do you know, Watson," said he, "that it is one of the curses of a mind with a turn like mine that I must look at everything with reference to my own special subject. You look at these scattered houses, and you are impressed by their beauty. I look at them, and the only thought which comes to me is a feeling of their isolation, and of the impunity with which crime may be committed there."

"The Adventure of the Copper Beeches" (1892)

APRIL 1

"THE GIANT RAT OF SUMATRA"

"Elementary, my dear Watson."

APRIL 2

"THE FIVE ORANGE PIPS" (1891)

"Why did you come to me," he cried, "and, above all, why did you not come at once?"

APRIL 3

"THE ADVENTURE OF THE SPECKLED BAND" (1892)

It was early in April in the year '83 that I woke one morning to find Sherlock Holmes standing, fully dressed, by the side of my bed. He was a late riser as a rule, and as the clock on the mantelpiece showed me that it was only a quarter-past seven, I blinked up at him in some surprise, and perhaps just a little resentment, for I was myself regular in my habits.

"By the way, Doctor, I shall want your co-operation."

"I shall be delighted."

"You don't mind breaking the law?"

"Not in the least."

"Nor running a chance of arrest?"

"Not in a good cause."

"Oh, the cause is excellent!"

"Then I am your man."

"I was sure that I might rely on you."

"Do you think he expects to make a success of it?"

"He has said nothing."

"That is a bad sign."

"On the contrary. I have noticed that when he is off the trail he generally says so. It is when he is on a scent and is not quite absolutely sure yet that it is the right one that he is most taciturn."

APRIL 6

"I am afraid that I rather give myself away when I explain," said he. "Results without causes are much more impressive."

APRIL 7

"I'm expecting something this evening."

"Expecting what?"

"To be murdered, Watson."

"No, no, you are joking, Holmes!"

"Even my limited sense of humour could evolve a better joke than that. But we may be comfortable in the meantime, may we not?"

APRIL 8

"I am glad to see that Mrs. Hudson has had the good sense to light the fire. Pray draw up to it, and I shall order you a cup of hot coffee, for I observe that you are shivering."

"It is not cold which makes me shiver," said the woman in a low voice, changing her seat as requested.

"What, then?"

"It is fear, Mr. Holmes. It is terror."

APRIL 9

A STUDY IN SCARLET (1887)

"Have you read Gaboriau's works?" I asked. "Does Lecoq come up to your idea of a detective?"

Sherlock Holmes sniffed sardonically. "Lecoq was a miserable bungler," he said, in an angry voice; "he had only one thing to recommend him, and that was his energy. That book made me positively ill. The question was how to identify an unknown prisoner. I could have done it in twenty-four hours. Lecoq took six months or so. It might be made a text-book for detectives to teach them what to avoid."

APRIL 10

"THE REIGATE SQUIRES" (1893)

"But this is what we really wanted." He held up a little crumpled piece of paper.

"The remainder of the sheet!" cried the inspector.

"Precisely."

"And where was it?"

"Where I was sure it must be."

Of all ruins, that of a noble mind is the most deplorable.

"The London criminal is certainly a dull fellow," said he in the querulous voice of the sportsman whose game has failed him. "Look out of this window, Watson. See how the figures loom up, are dimly seen, and then blend once more into the cloud-bank. The thief or the murderer could roam London on such a day as the tiger does the jungle, unseen until he pounces, and then evident only to his victim."

"There have," said I, "been numerous petty thefts."

Holmes snorted his contempt.

"This great and sombre stage is set for something more worthy than that," said he. "It is fortunate for this community that I am not a criminal."

THE VALLEY OF FEAR (1915)

"Well, Holmes," I murmured, "have you found any-thing out?"

He stood beside me in silence, his candle in his hand. Then the tall, lean figure inclined towards me. "I say, Watson," he whispered, "would you be afraid to sleep in the same room with a lunatic, a man with softening of the brain, an idiot whose mind has lost its grip?"

"Not in the least," I answered in astonishment.

"Ah, that's lucky," he said, and not another word would he utter that night.

"THE REIGATE SQUIRES" (1893)

On referring to my notes I see that it was upon the fourteenth of April that I received a telegram from Lyons which informed me that Holmes was lying ill in the Hotel Dulong. Within twenty-four hours I was in his sick-room and was relieved to find that there was nothing formidable in his symptoms. Even his iron constitution, however, had broken down under the strain of an investigation which had extended over two months, during which period he had never worked less than fifteen hours a day and had more than once, as he assured me, kept to his task for five days at a stretch. Even the triumphant issue of his labours could not save him from reaction after so terrible an exertion, and at a time when Europe was ringing with his name and when his room was literally ankle-deep with congratulatory telegrams I found him a prey to the blackest depression. Even the knowledge that he had succeeded where the police of three countries had failed, and that he had out-manoeuvred at every point the most accomplished swindler in Europe, was insufficient to rouse him from his nervous prostration.

APRIL 15

THE HOUND OF THE BASKERVILLES (1902)

"One last question, Holmes," I said as I rose. "Surely there is no need of secrecy between you and me. What is the meaning of it all? What is he after?"

Holmes's voice sank as he answered:

"It is murder, Watson—refined, cold-blooded, deliberate murder."

APRIL 16

THE SIGN OF FOUR (1890)

At Greenwich we were about three hundred paces behind them. At Blackwall we could not have been more than two hundred and fifty. I have coursed many creatures in many countries during my checkered career, but never did sport give me such a wild thrill as this mad, flying man-hunt down the Thames.

APRIL 17

"THE ADVENTURE OF
THE NORWOOD BUILDER" (1903)

"You mentioned your name, as if I should recognise it, but I assure you that, beyond the obvious facts that you are a bachelor, a solicitor, a Freemason, and an asthmatic, I know nothing whatever about you."

Familiar as I was with my friend's methods, it was not difficult for me to follow his deductions, and to observe the untidiness of attire, the sheaf of legal papers, the watch-charm, and the breathing which had prompted them. Our client, however, stared in amazement.

APRIL 18

THE VALLEY OF FEAR (1915)

Mediocrity knows nothing higher than itself; but talent instantly recognizes genius.

APRIL 19

"There are only those three capable of playing so bold a game—there are Oberstein, La Rothière, and Eduardo Lucas. I will see each of them."

I glanced at my morning paper.

"Is that Eduardo Lucas of Godolphin Street?"

"Yes."

"You will not see him."

"Why not?"

"He was murdered in his house last night."

My friend has so often astonished me in the course of our adventures that it was with a sense of exultation that I realized how completely I had astonished him.

APRIL 20

"What do you make of it, Watson?"

"A cipher message, Holmes."

My companion gave a sudden chuckle of comprehension. "And not a very obscure cipher, Watson," said he. "Why, of course, it is Italian!"

"The more *outré* and grotesque an incident is the more carefully it deserves to be examined, and the very point which appears to complicate a case is, when duly considered and scientifically handled, the one which is most likely to elucidate it."

"Have you the effrontery necessary to put it through?"

"We can but try."

"Excellent, Watson! Compound of the Busy Bee and Excelsior. We can but try—the motto of the firm."

I am certainly developing the wisdom of the serpent, for when Mortimer pressed his questions to an inconvenient extent I asked him casually to what type Frankland's skull belonged, and so heard nothing but craniology for the rest of our drive. I have not lived for years with Sherlock Holmes for nothing.

APRIL 24

"I think that you know me well enough, Watson, to understand that I am by no means a nervous man. At the same time, it is stupidity rather than courage to refuse to recognize danger when it is close upon you."

APRIL 25
"THE CARDBOARD BOX" (1893)

"The features are given to man as the means by which he shall express his emotions, and yours are faithful servants."

APRIL 26
"THE MAN WITH THE TWISTED LIP" (1891)

"You have a grand gift of silence, Watson," said he. "It makes you quite invaluable as a companion."

APRIL 27
"THE ADVENTURE OF THE DYING DETECTIVE" (1913)

I have so deep a respect for the extraordinary qualities of Holmes that I have always deferred to his wishes, even when I least understood them. But now all my professional instincts were aroused. Let him be my master elsewhere, I at least was his in a sick room.

APRIL 28

"THE CARDBOARD BOX" (1893)

"You remember," said he, "that some little time ago when I read you the passage in one of Poe's sketches in which a close reasoner follows the unspoken thoughts of his companion, you were inclined to treat the matter as a mere *tour-de-force* of the author. On my remarking that I was constantly in the habit of doing the same thing you expressed incredulity."

"Oh, no!"

"Perhaps not with your tongue, my dear Watson, but certainly with your eyebrows."

APRIL 29

"THE ADVENTURE OF THE EMPTY HOUSE" (1903)

"There are some trees, Watson, which grow to a certain height, and then suddenly develop some unsightly eccentricity. You will see it often in humans. I have a theory that the individual represents in his development the whole procession of his ancestors, and that such a sudden turn to good or evil stands for some strong influence which came into the line of his pedigree. The person becomes, as it were, the epitome of the history of his own family."

"It is surely rather fanciful."

"Well, I don't insist upon it."

APRIL 30

"THE MAN WITH THE TWISTED LIP" (1891)

"I am sure, Mr. Holmes, that we are very much indebted to you for having cleared the matter up. I wish I knew how you reach your results."

"I reached this one," said my friend, "by sitting upon five pillows and consuming an ounce of shag. I think, Watson, that if we drive to Baker Street we shall just be in time for breakfast."

MAY

A rainy night had been followed by a glorious morning, and the heath-covered countryside, with the glowing clumps of flowering gorse, seemed all the more beautiful to eyes which were weary of the duns and drabs and slate greys of London. Holmes and I walked along the broad, sandy road inhaling the fresh morning air and rejoicing in the music of the birds and the fresh breath of the spring.

"The Adventure of the Solitary Cyclist" (1903)

MAY 1

"I shall glance into the case for you," said Holmes, rising, "and I have no doubt that we shall reach some definite result. Let the weight of the matter rest upon me now, and do not let your mind dwell upon it further."

MAY 2

"But I have heard, Mr. Holmes, that you can see deeply into the manifold wickedness of the human heart. You may advise me how to walk amid the dangers which encompass me."

MAY 3

It was on the third of May that we reached the little village of Meiringen, where we put up at the Englischer Hof, then kept by Peter Steiler the elder. Our landlord was an intelligent man and spoke excellent English, having served for three years as waiter at the Grosvenor Hotel in London. At his advice, on the afternoon of the fourth we set off together, with the intention of crossing the hills and spending the night at the hamlet of Rosenlaui. We had strict injunctions, however, on no account to pass the falls of Reichenbach, which are about halfway up the hills, without making a small detour to see them.

MAY 4

"THE FINAL PROBLEM" (1893)

As I turned away, I saw Holmes, with his back against a rock and his arms folded, gazing down at the rush of the waters. It was the last that I was ever destined to see of him in this world.

MAY 5

"THE ADVENTURE OF THE EMPTY HOUSE" (1903)

"The instant that the Professor had disappeared, it struck me what a really extraordinarily lucky chance Fate had placed in my way. I knew that Moriarty was not the only man who had sworn my death. There were at least three others whose desire for vengeance upon me would only be increased by the death of their leader. They were all most dangerous men. One or other would certainly get me. On the other hand, if all the world was convinced that I was dead they would take liberties, these men, they would soon lay themselves open, and sooner or later I could destroy them. Then it would be time for me to announce that I was still in the land of the living. So rapidly does the brain act that I believe I had thought this all out before Professor Moriarty had reached the bottom of the Reichenbach Fall."

MAY 6
"THE YELLOW FACE" (1893)

"Pipes are occasionally of extraordinary interest," said he. "Nothing has more individuality, save perhaps watches and bootlaces."

MAY 7
"THE ADVENTURE OF CHARLES AUGUSTUS MILVERTON" (1904)

"We have shared this same room for some years, and it would be amusing if we ended by sharing the same cell."

MAY 8
"THE ADVENTURE OF THE RED CIRCLE" (1911)

Our official detectives may blunder in the matter of intelligence, but never in that of courage. Gregson climbed the stair to arrest this desperate murderer with the same absolutely quiet and businesslike bearing with which he would have ascended the official staircase of Scotland Yard. The Pinkerton man had tried to push past him, but Gregson had firmly elbowed him back. London dangers were the privilege of the London force.

MAY 9
"THE ADVENTURE OF THE COPPER BEECHES" (1892)

"It is my belief, Watson, founded upon my experience, that the lowest and vilest alleys in London do not present a more dreadful record of sin than does the smiling and beautiful countryside."

MAY 10
"THE ADVENTURE OF THE BLUE CARBUNCLE" (1892)

"Then, what clue could you have as to his identity?"

"Only as much as we can deduce."

"From his hat?"

"Precisely."

MAY 11

"Depend upon it, there is nothing so unnatural as the commonplace."

MAY 12

Sherlock Holmes was a man who seldom took exercise for exercise's sake. Few men were capable of greater muscular effort, and he was undoubtedly one of the finest boxers of his weight that I have ever seen; but he looked upon aimless bodily exertion as a waste of energy, and he seldom bestirred himself save where there was some professional object to be served. Then he was absolutely untiring and indefatigable. That he should have kept himself in training under such circumstances is remarkable, but his diet was usually of the sparest, and his habits were simple to the verge of austerity. Save for the occasional use of cocaine, he had no vices, and he only turned to the drug as a protest against the monotony of existence when cases were scanty and the papers uninteresting.

MAY 13

Indeed, apart from the nature of the investigation which my friend had on hand, there was something in his masterly grasp of a situation, and his keen, incisive reasoning, which made it a pleasure to me to study his system of work, and to follow the quick, subtle methods by which he disentangled the most inextricable mysteries. So accustomed was I to his invariable success that the very possibility of his failing had ceased to enter into my head.

MAY 14

"THE DISAPPEARANCE OF
LADY FRANCES CARFAX" (1911)

"Besides, on general principles it is best that I should not leave the country. Scotland Yard feels lonely without me, and it causes an unhealthy excitement among the criminal classes."

"Remarkable!" he said, when the story was unfolded, "most remarkable! I can hardly recall any case where the features have been more peculiar."

"I thought you would say so, Mr. Holmes," said White Mason in great delight. "We're well up with the times in Sussex."

"I trust that there is nothing of consequence which I have overlooked?"

"I am afraid, my dear Watson, that most of your conclusions were erroneous. When I said that you stimulated me I meant, to be frank, that in noting your fallacies I was occasionally guided towards the truth."

"Then, pray tell me what it is that you can infer from this hat?"

He picked it up and gazed at it in the peculiar introspective fashion which was characteristic of him. "It is perhaps less suggestive than it might have been," he remarked, "and yet there are a few inferences which are very distinct, and a few others which represent at least a strong balance of probability. That the man was highly intellectual is of course obvious upon the face of it, and also that he was fairly well-to-do within the last three years, although he has now fallen upon evil days. He had foresight, but has less now than formerly, pointing to a moral retrogression, which, when taken with the decline of his fortunes, seems to indicate some evil influence, probably drink, at work upon him. This may account also for the obvious fact that his wife has ceased to love him."

"My dear Holmes!"

MAY 18

"THE ADVENTURE OF THE SPECKLED BAND" (1892)

"Indeed," said Holmes. "Was it your custom always to lock yourselves in at night?"

"Always."

"And why?"

"I think that I mentioned to you that the doctor kept a cheetah and a baboon. We had no feeling of security unless our doors were locked."

"Quite so."

"A dog reflects the family life. Whoever saw a frisky dog in a gloomy family, or a sad dog in a happy one? Snarling people have snarling dogs, dangerous people have dangerous ones."

"And the dog?"

"Has been in the habit of carrying this stick behind his master. Being a heavy stick the dog has held it tightly by the middle, and the marks of his teeth are very plainly visible. The dog's jaw, as shown in the space between these marks, is too broad in my opinion for a terrier and not broad enough for a mastiff. It may have been—yes, by Jove, it *is* a curly-haired spaniel."

He had risen and paced the room as he spoke. Now he halted in the recess of the window. There was such a ring of conviction in his voice that I glanced up in surprise.

"My dear fellow, how can you possibly be so sure of that?"

"For the very simple reason that I see the dog himself on our very door-step."

MAY 21

THE SIGN OF FOUR (1890)

"You will bring Toby back in the cab with you."

"A dog, I suppose."

"Yes, a queer mongrel with a most amazing power of scent. I would rather have Toby's help than that of the whole detective force of London."

MAY 22

"SILVER BLAZE" (1892)

"Is there any point to which you would wish to draw my attention?"

"To the curious incident of the dog in the night-time."

"The dog did nothing in the night-time."

"That was the curious incident," remarked Sherlock Holmes.

MAY 23

"THE ADVENTURE OF THE MISSING THREE-QUARTER" (1904)

"I do not know whether it came from his own innate depravity or from the promptings of his master, but he was rude enough to set a dog at me. Neither dog nor man liked the look of my stick, however, and the matter fell through. Relations were strained after that, and further inquiries out of the question."

"THE ADVENTURE OF CHARLES AUGUSTUS
MILVERTON" (1904)

I knew that the opening of safes was a particular hobby with him, and I understood the joy which it gave him to be confronted with this green and gold monster, the dragon which held in its maw the reputations of many fair ladies.

MAY 25

A STUDY IN SCARLET (1887)

"I have already explained to you that what is out of the common is usually a guide rather than a hindrance. In solving a problem of this sort, the grand thing is to be able to reason backward. That is a very useful accomplishment, and a very easy one, but people do not practise it much. In the everyday affairs of life it is more useful to reason forward, and so the other comes to be neglected. There are fifty who can reason synthetically for one who can reason analytically."

MAY 26

"THE ADVENTURE OF THE SPECKLED BAND" (1892)

"As I bent over her she suddenly shrieked out in a voice which I shall never forget, 'Oh, my God! Helen! It was the band! The speckled band!'"

MAY 27

THE SIGN OF FOUR (1890)

"He speaks as a pupil to his master," said I.

"Oh, he rates my assistance too highly," said Sherlock Holmes lightly. "He has considerable gifts himself. He possesses two out of the three qualities necessary for the ideal detective. He has the power of observation and that of deduction. He is only wanting in knowledge, and that may come in time."

MAY 28

THE HOUND OF THE BASKERVILLES (1902)

"My eyes have been trained to examine faces and not their trimmings. It is the first quality of a criminal investigator that he should see through a disguise."

A problem without a solution may interest the student, but can hardly fail to annoy the casual reader.

"You see, the whole thing is a chain of logical sequences without a break or flaw."

"It is wonderful!" I cried. "Your merits should be publicly recognized. You should publish an account of the case. If you won't, I will for you."

"You may do what you like, Doctor," he answered.

"Mr. Holmes, you are a wizard, a sorcerer! How did you know it was there?"

"Because I knew it was nowhere else."

JUNE

"How sweet the morning air is! See how that one little cloud floats like a pink feather from some gigantic flamingo. Now the red rim of the sun pushes itself over the London cloud-bank. It shines on a good many folk, but on none, I dare bet, who are on a stranger errand than you and I. How small we feel with our petty ambitions and strivings in the presence of the great elemental forces of Nature!"

The Sign of Four (1890)

JUNE 1

"You then went to the vicarage, waited outside it for some time, and finally returned to your cottage."

"How do you know that?"

"I followed you."

"I saw no one."

"That is what you may expect to see when I follow you."

JUNE 2

"I have had to move into the chamber in which my sister died, and to sleep in the very bed in which she slept. Imagine, then, my thrill of terror when last night, as I lay awake, thinking over her terrible fate, I suddenly heard in the silence of the night the low whistle which had been the herald of her own death."

JUNE 3

"On June 3, that is, on Monday last, McCarthy left his house at Hatherley about three in the afternoon and walked down to the Boscombe Pool, which is a small lake formed by the spreading out of the stream which runs down the Boscombe Valley. He had been out with his serving-man in the morning at Ross, and he had told the man that he must hurry, as he had an appointment of importance to keep at three. From that appointment he never came back alive."

JUNE 4
"A CASE OF IDENTITY" (1891)

"'Pon my word, Watson, you are coming along wonderfully. You have really done very well indeed. It is true that you have missed everything of importance, but you have hit upon the method, and you have a quick eye for colour. Never trust to general impressions, my boy, but concentrate yourself upon details."

JUNE 5
"THE ADVENTURE OF THE EMPTY HOUSE" (1903)

"That you, Lestrade?" said Holmes.

"Yes, Mr. Holmes. I took the job myself. It's good to see you back in London, sir."

"I think you want a little unofficial help. Three undetected murders in one year won't do, Lestrade. But you handled the Molesey Mystery with less than your usual—that's to say, you handled it fairly well."

JUNE 6

"Here is a very fashionable epistle," I remarked as he entered. "Your morning letters, if I remember right, were from a fishmonger and a tide waiter."

"Yes, my correspondence has certainly the charm of variety."

JUNE 7

Holmes took up the stone and held it against the light. "It's a bonny thing," said he. "Just see how it glints and sparkles. Of course it is a nucleus and focus of crime. Every good stone is. They are the devil's pet baits. In the larger and older jewels every facet may stand for a bloody deed."

JUNE 8

"When you combine the ideas of whistles at night, the presence of a band of gipsies who are on intimate terms with this old Doctor, the fact that we have every reason to believe that the Doctor has an interest in preventing his stepdaughter's marriage, the dying allusion to a band, and, finally, the fact that Miss Helen Stoner heard a metallic clang, which might have been caused by one of those metal bars which secured the shutters falling back into its place, I think that there is good ground to think that the mystery may be cleared along those lines."

JUNE 9

THE VALLEY OF FEAR (1915)

Three centuries had flowed past the old Manor House, centuries of births and of homecomings, of country dances and of the meetings of fox hunters. Strange that now in its old age this dark business should have cast its shadow upon the venerable walls! And yet those strange, peaked roofs and quaint, overhung gables were a fitting covering to grim and terrible intrigue. As I looked at the deep-set windows and the long sweep of the dull-coloured, water-lapped front, I felt that no more fitting scene could be set for such a tragedy.

JUNE 10

"THE ADVENTURE OF THE RED CIRCLE" (1911)

"The matches have, of course, been used to light cigarettes. That is obvious from the shortness of the burnt end. Half the match is consumed in lighting a pipe or cigar. But, dear me! this cigarette stub is certainly remarkable. The gentleman was bearded and moustached, you say?"

"Yes, sir."

"I don't understand that. I should say that only a clean-shaven man could have smoked this. Why, Watson, even your modest moustache would have been singed."

"A holder?" I suggested.

"No, no; the end is matted."

JUNE 11

"THE MAN WITH THE TWISTED LIP" (1891)

"I perceive also that whoever addressed the envelope had to go and inquire as to the address."

"How can you tell that?"

"The name, you see, is in perfectly black ink, which has dried itself. The rest is of the greyish colour, which shows that the blotting-paper has been used. If it had been written straight off, and then blotted, none would be of a deep black shade. This man has written the name, and there has then been a pause before he wrote the address, which can only mean that he was not familiar with it. It is, of course, a trifle, but there is nothing so important as trifles."

"But I assure you you are mistaken about my alleged agents."

Count Sylvius laughed contemptuously.

"Other people can observe as well as you. Yesterday there was an old sporting man. To-day it was an elderly woman. They held me in view all day."

"Really, sir, you compliment me. Old Baron Dowson said the night before he was hanged that in my case what the law had gained the stage had lost. And now you give my little impersonations your kindly praise?"

"It was you—you yourself?"

Holmes shrugged his shoulders. "You can see in the corner the parasol which you so politely handed to me in the Minories before you began to suspect."

"You are proud of your brains, Holmes, are you not? Think yourself smart, don't you? You came across someone who was smarter this time."

JUNE 14

A STUDY IN SCARLET (1887)

"This fellow may be very clever," I said to myself, "but he is certainly very conceited."

JUNE 15

"THE MAN WITH THE TWISTED LIP" (1891)

One night—it was in June, '89—there came a ring to my bell, about the hour when a man gives his first yawn and glances at the clock.

JUNE 16

"THE ADVENTURE OF THE CREEPING MAN" (1923)

"Always look at the hands first, Watson. Then cuffs, trouser-knees, and boots."

JUNE 17

A STUDY IN SCARLET (1887)

"You remind me of Edgar Allan Poe's Dupin. I had no idea that such individuals did exist outside of stories."

Sherlock Holmes rose and lit his pipe. "No doubt you think that you are complimenting me in comparing me to Dupin," he observed. "Now, in my opinion, Dupin was a very inferior fellow. That trick of his of breaking in on his friends' thoughts with an apropos remark after a quarter of an hour's silence is really very showy and superficial. He had some analytical genius, no doubt; but he was by no means such a phenomenon as Poe appeared to imagine."

JUNE 18

"THE ADVENTURE OF THE SECOND STAIN" (1904)

"Only one important thing has happened in the last three days, and that is that nothing has happened."

JUNE 19

"THE ADVENTURE OF BLACK PETER" (1904)

Holmes, however, like all great artists, lived for his art's sake, and, save in the case of the Duke of Holdernesse, I have seldom known him claim any large reward for his inestimable services. So unworldly was he—or so capricious—that he frequently refused his help to the powerful and wealthy where the problem made no appeal to his sympathies, while he would devote weeks of most intense application to the affairs of some humble client whose case presented those strange and dramatic qualities which appealed to his imagination and challenged his ingenuity.

JUNE 20

THE SIGN OF FOUR (1890)

"Yes, I have been guilty of several monographs. They are all upon technical subjects. Here, for example, is one 'Upon the Distinction between the Ashes of the Various Tobaccos.' In it I enumerate a hundred and forty forms of cigar, cigarette, and pipe tobacco, with coloured plates illustrating the difference in the ash. It is a point which is continually turning up in criminal trials, and which is sometimes of supreme importance as a clue. If you can say definitely, for example, that some murder had been done by a man who was smoking an Indian lunkah, it obviously narrows your field of search. To the trained eye there is as much difference between the black ash of a Trichinopoly and the white fluff of bird's-eye as there is between a cabbage and a potato."

"You have an extraordinary genius for minutiae," I remarked.

"I appreciate their importance."

His ignorance was as remarkable as his knowledge. Of contemporary literature, philosophy and politics he appeared to know next to nothing. Upon my quoting Thomas Carlyle, he inquired in the naivest way who he might be and what he had done. My surprise reached a climax, however, when I found incidentally that he was ignorant of the Copernican Theory and of the composition of the Solar System. That any civilized human being in this nineteenth century should not be aware that the earth travelled round the sun appeared to be to me such an extraordinary fact that I could hardly realize it.

JUNE 22

"THE ADVENTURE OF
THE ENGINEER'S THUMB" (1892)

The story has, I believe, been told more than once in the newspapers, but, like all such narratives, its effect is much less striking when set forth *en bloc* in a single half-column of print than when the facts slowly evolve before your own eyes, and the mystery clears gradually away as each new discovery furnishes a step which leads on to the complete truth.

JUNE 23

A STUDY IN SCARLET (1887)

During the first week or so we had no callers, and I had begun to think that my companion was as friendless a man as I was myself. Presently, however, I found that he had many acquaintances, and those in the most different classes of society. There was one little sallow rat-faced, dark-eyed fellow, who was introduced to me as Mr. Lestrade, and who came three or four times in a single week.

JUNE 24

A STUDY IN SCARLET (1887)

Gregson and Lestrade had watched the manoeuvres of their amateur companion with considerable curiosity and some contempt. They evidently failed to appreciate the fact, which I had begun to realize, that Sherlock Holmes's smallest actions were all directed towards some definite and practical end.

"What do you think of it, sir?" they both asked.

"It should be robbing you of the credit of the case if I was to presume to help you," remarked my friend. "You are doing so well now that it would be a pity for anyone to interfere." There was a world of sarcasm in his voice as he spoke.

JUNE 25

"We have got to the deductions and the inferences," said Lestrade, winking at me. "I find it hard enough to tackle facts, Holmes, without flying away after theories and fancies."

"You are right," said Holmes demurely; "you do find it very hard to tackle the facts."

JUNE 26

The London express came roaring into the station, and a small, wiry bulldog of a man had sprung from a first-class carriage. We all three shook hands, and I saw at once from the reverential way in which Lestrade gazed at my companion that he had learned a good deal since the days when they had first worked together. I could well remember the scorn which the theories of the reasoner used then to excite in the practical man.

JUNE 27

It was no very unusual thing for Mr. Lestrade, of Scotland Yard, to look in upon us of an evening, and his visits were welcome to Sherlock Holmes, for they enabled him to keep in touch with all that was going on at the police headquarters. In return for the news which Lestrade would bring, Holmes was always ready to listen with attention to the details of any case upon which the detective was engaged, and was able occasionally, without any active interference, to give some hint or suggestion drawn from his own vast knowledge and experience.

JUNE 28

THE HOUND OF THE BASKERVILLES (1902)

"Are you armed, Lestrade?"

The little detective smiled.

"As long as I have my trousers I have a hip-pocket, and as long as I have my hip-pocket I have something in it."

JUNE 29

"THE ADVENTURE OF
THE NORWOOD BUILDER" (1903)

At one end of the corridor we were all marshalled by Sherlock Holmes, the constables grinning and Lestrade staring at my friend with amazement, expectation, and derision chasing each other across his features. Holmes stood before us with the air of a conjurer who is performing a trick.

JUNE 30

"THE ADVENTURE OF THE SIX NAPOLEONS" (1904)

"Well," said Lestrade, "I've seen you handle a good many cases, Mr. Holmes, but I don't know that I ever knew a more workmanlike one than that. We're not jealous of you at Scotland Yard. No, sir, we are very proud of you, and if you come down to-morrow, there's not a man, from the oldest inspector to the youngest constable, who wouldn't be glad to shake you by the hand."

"Thank you!" said Holmes. "Thank you!" and as he turned away, it seemed to me that he was more nearly moved by the softer human emotions than I had ever seen him. A moment later he was the cold and practical thinker once more.

JULY

During the first week of July, my friend had been absent so often and so long from our lodgings that I knew he had something on hand. The fact that several rough-looking men called during that time and inquired for Captain Basil made me understand that Holmes was working somewhere under one of the numerous disguises and names with which he concealed his own formidable identity.

"The Adventure of Black Peter" (1904)

"If this young person should produce her letters for blackmailing or other purposes, how is she to prove their authenticity?"

"There is the writing."

"Pooh, pooh! Forgery."

"My private note-paper."

"Stolen."

"My own seal."

"Imitated."

"My photograph."

"Bought."

"We were both in the photograph."

"Oh, dear! That is very bad! Your Majesty has indeed committed an indiscretion."

"Between ourselves, I think Mr. Holmes has not quite got over his illness yet. He's been behaving very queerly, and he is very much excited."

"I don't think you need alarm yourself," said I. "I have usually found that there was method in his madness."

"Some folk might say there was madness in his method."

JULY 3

"Really, Watson, you excel yourself," said Holmes, pushing back his chair and lighting a cigarette. "I am bound to say that in all the accounts which you have been so good as to give of my own small achievements you have habitually underrated your own abilities. It may be that you are not yourself luminous, but you are a conductor of light. Some people without possessing genius have a remarkable power of stimulating it. I confess, my dear fellow, that I am very much in your debt."

JULY 4

"There was no complete maker's name; but the printed letters 'P-E-N' were on the fluting between the barrels, and the rest of the name had been cut off by the saw."

"A big 'P' with a flourish above it, 'E' and 'N' smaller?" asked Holmes.

"Exactly."

"Pennsylvania Small Arms Company—well-known American firm," said Holmes.

White Mason gazed at my friend as the little village practitioner looks at the Harley Street specialist who by a word can solve the difficulties that perplex him.

JULY 5

To Holmes, as I could see by his eager face and peering eyes, very many other things were to be read upon the trampled grass. He ran round, like a dog who is picking up a scent.

JULY 6

"Any truth is better than indefinite doubt."

JULY 7

"This morning I received this letter, which you will perhaps read for yourself."

"Thank you," said Holmes. "The envelope, too, please. Post-mark, London, S. W. Date, July 7. Hum! Man's thumb-mark on corner—probably postman. Best quality paper. Envelopes at sixpence a packet. Particular man in his stationery. No address. 'Be at the third pillar from the left outside the Lyceum Theatre to-night at seven o'clock. If you are distrustful bring two friends. You are a wronged woman and shall have justice. Do not bring police. If you do, all will be in vain. Your unknown friend.' Well, really, this is a very pretty mystery! What do you intend to do, Miss Morstan?"

JULY 8

A STUDY IN SCARLET (1887)

"There is a mystery about this which stimulates the imagination; where there is no imagination there is no horror."

JULY 9

"SILVER BLAZE" (1892)

"It is one of those cases where the art of the reasoner should be used rather for the sifting of details than for the acquiring of fresh evidence. The tragedy has been so uncommon, so complete, and of such personal importance to so many people that we are suffering from a plethora of surmise, conjecture, and hypothesis. The difficulty is to detach the framework of fact—of absolute undeniable fact—from the embellishments of theorists and reporters. Then, having established ourselves upon this sound basis, it is our duty to see what inferences may be drawn and what are the special points upon which the whole mystery turns."

JULY 10

"THE GREEK INTERPRETER" (1893)

"My dear Watson," said he, "I cannot agree with those who rank modesty among the virtues. To the logician all things should be seen exactly as they are, and to underestimate one's self is as much a departure from truth as to exaggerate one's own powers. When I say, therefore, that Mycroft has better powers of observation than I, you may take it that I am speaking the exact and literal truth."

JULY 11

A STUDY IN SCARLET (1887)

"I should have more faith," he said; "I ought to know by this time that when a fact appears to be opposed to a long train of deductions, it invariably proves to be capable of bearing some other interpretation."

JULY 12

"THE BOSCOMBE VALLEY MYSTERY" (1891)

Sherlock Holmes was transformed when he was hot upon such a scent as this. Men who had only known the quiet thinker and logician of Baker Street would have failed to recognize him. His face flushed and darkened. His brows were drawn into two hard black lines, while his eyes shone out from beneath them with a steely glitter. His face was bent downward, his shoulders bowed, his lips compressed, and the veins stood out like whipcord in his long, sinewy neck. His nostrils seemed to dilate with a purely animal lust for the chase, and his mind was so absolutely concentrated upon the matter before him that a question or remark fell unheeded upon his ears, or, at the most, only provoked a quick, impatient snarl in reply.

JULY 13

"THE ADVENTURE OF THE MISSING THREE-QUARTER" (1904)

A cold supper was ready upon the table, and when his needs were satisfied and his pipe alight he was ready to take that half comic and wholly philosophic view which was natural to him when his affairs were going awry.

JULY 14

"THE ADVENTURE OF THE ABBEY GRANGE" (1904)

"Be frank with me and we may do some good. Play tricks with me, and I'll crush you."

THE SIGN OF FOUR (1890)

He whipped out his lens and a tape measure and hurried about the room on his knees, measuring, comparing, examining, with his long thin nose only a few inches from the planks and his beady eyes gleaming and deep-set like those of a bird. So swift, silent, and furtive were his movements, like those of a trained bloodhound picking out a scent, that I could not but think what a terrible criminal he would have made had he turned his energy and sagacity against the law instead of exerting them in its defence.

JULY 16

"THE ADVENTURE OF THE SPECKLED BAND" (1892)

"Ha! You put me off, do you?" said our new visitor, taking a step forward and shaking his hunting-crop. "I know you, you scoundrel! I have heard of you before. You are Holmes the meddler."

My friend smiled.

"Holmes the busybody!"

His smile broadened.

"Holmes the Scotland Yard Jack-in-office!"

Holmes chuckled heartily. "Your conversation is most entertaining," said he. "When you go out close the door, for there is a decided draught."

JULY 17

THE VALLEY OF FEAR (1915)

It was one of those dramatic moments for which my friend existed. It would be an overstatement to say that he was shocked or even excited by the amazing announcement. Without having a tinge of cruelty in his singular composition, he was undoubtedly callous from long overstimulation. Yet, if his emotions were dulled, his intellectual perceptions were exceedingly active. There was no trace then of the horror which I had myself felt at this curt declaration; but his face showed rather the quiet and interested composure of the chemist who sees the crystals falling into position from his oversaturated solution.

JULY 18

"THE DISAPPEARANCE OF
LADY FRANCES CARFAX" (1911)

My companion started. "Well?" he asked, in that vibrant voice which told of the fiery soul behind the cold grey face.

JULY 19

"All knowledge comes useful to the detective."

JULY 20

"THE ADVENTURE OF THE SPECKLED BAND" (1892)

"I am a dangerous man to fall foul of! See here." He stepped swiftly forward, seized the poker, and bent it into a curve with his huge brown hands.

"See that you keep yourself out of my grip," he snarled, and hurling the twisted poker into the fireplace, he strode out of the room.

"He seems a very amiable person," said Holmes, laughing. "I am not quite so bulky, but if he had remained I might have shown him that my grip was not much more feeble than his own." As he spoke he picked up the steel poker and, with a sudden effort, straightened it out again.

JULY 21

"THE ADVENTURE OF THE EMPTY HOUSE" (1903)

"Just give me down my index of biographies from the shelf."

He turned over the pages lazily, leaning back in

his chair and blowing great clouds from his cigar.

"My collection of M's is a fine one," said he. "Moriarty himself is enough to make any letter illustrious, and here is Morgan the poisoner, and Merridew of abominable memory, and Mathews, who knocked out my left canine in the waiting-room at Charing Cross."

JULY 22

THE SIGN OF FOUR (1890)

"He had doubtless planned beforehand that, should he slay the major, he would leave some such record upon the body as a sign that it was not a common murder but, from the point of view of the four associates, something in the nature of an act of justice. Whimsical and bizarre conceits of this kind are common enough in the annals of crime and usually afford valuable indications as to the criminal."

JULY 23

THE HOUND OF THE BASKERVILLES (1902)

"The world is full of obvious things which nobody by any chance ever observes."

JULY 24

"I should be very much obliged if you would slip your revolver into your pocket. An Eley's No. 2 is an excellent argument with gentlemen who can twist steel pokers into knots. That and a tooth-brush are, I think, all that we need."

JULY 25

"The past and the present are within the field of my inquiry, but what a man may do in the future is a hard question to answer."

JULY 26

I trust that I am not more dense than my neighbours, but I was always oppressed with a sense of my own stupidity in my dealings with Sherlock Holmes.

JULY 27

"You see, but you do not observe. The distinction is clear. For example, you have frequently seen the steps which lead up from the hall to this room."

"Frequently."

"How often?"

"Well, some hundreds of times."

"Then how many are there?"

"How many? I don't know."

"Quite so! You have not observed. And yet you have seen. That is just my point."

JULY 28

"The detection of types is one of the most elementary branches of knowledge to the special expert in crime, though I confess that once when I was very young I confused the *Leeds Mercury* with the *Western Morning News*."

JULY 29

I spent a few minutes in assisting a venerable Italian priest, who was endeavouring to make a porter understand, in his broken English, that his luggage was to be booked through to Paris. Then, having taken another look round, I returned to my carriage, where I found that the porter, in spite of the ticket, had given me my decrepit Italian friend as a travelling companion. It was useless for me to explain to him that his presence was an intrusion, for my Italian was even more limited than his English, so I shrugged my shoulders resignedly, and continued to look out anxiously for my friend. A chill of fear had come over me, as I thought that his absence might mean that some blow had fallen during the night. Already the doors had all been shut and the whistle blown, when—

"My dear Watson," said a voice, "you have not even condescended to say good-morning."

I turned in uncontrollable astonishment. The aged ecclesiastic had turned his face towards me. For an instant the wrinkles were smoothed away, the nose drew away from the chin, the lower lip ceased to protrude and the mouth to mumble, the dull eyes regained their fire, the drooping figure expanded. The next the whole frame collapsed again, and Holmes had gone as quickly as he had come.

JULY 30
A STUDY IN SCARLET (1887)

"All this seems strange to you," continued Holmes, "because you failed at the beginning of the inquiry to grasp the importance of the single real clue which was presented to you. I had the good fortune to seize upon that, and everything which has occurred since then has served to confirm my original supposition, and, indeed, was the logical sequence of it."

JULY 31
"THE FIVE ORANGE PIPS" (1891)

Sherlock Holmes was able, by winding up the dead man's watch, to prove that it had been wound up two hours before, and that therefore the deceased had gone to bed within that time—a deduction which was of the greatest importance in clearing up the case.

AUGUST

It was a blazing hot day in August. Baker Street was like an oven, and the glare of the sunlight upon the yellow brickwork of the house across the road was painful to the eye. It was hard to believe that these were the same walls which loomed so gloomily through the fogs of winter. Our blinds were half-drawn, and Holmes lay curled upon the sofa, reading and re-reading a letter which he had received by the morning post. For myself, my term of service in India had trained me to stand heat better than cold, and a thermometer at ninety was no hardship.

"The Cardboard Box" (1893)

AUGUST 1

"My dear Watson, you know how bored I have been since we locked up Colonel Carruthers. My mind is like a racing engine, tearing itself to pieces because it is not connected up with the work for which it was built. Life is commonplace; the papers are sterile; audacity and romance seem to have passed forever from the criminal world. Can you ask me, then, whether I am ready to look into any new problem, however trivial it may prove?"

AUGUST 2

It was nine o'clock at night upon the second of August—the most terrible August in the history of the world. One might have thought already that God's curse hung heavy over a degenerate world, for there was an awesome hush and a feeling of vague expectancy in the sultry and stagnant air.

AUGUST 3

"A cast of your skull, sir, until the original is available, would be an ornament to any anthropological museum. It is not my intention to be fulsome, but I confess that I covet your skull."

Sherlock Holmes waved our strange visitor into a chair. "You are an enthusiast in your line of thought, I perceive, sir, as I am in mine."

AUGUST 4

"THE ADVENTURE OF THE SPECKLED BAND" (1892)

"Ah, me! it's a wicked world, and when a clever man turns his brains to crime it is the worst of all."

AUGUST 5

"THE RED-HEADED LEAGUE" (1891)

"My dear doctor, this is a time for observation, not for talk. We are spies in an enemy's country."

AUGUST 6

"THE BOSCOMBE VALLEY MYSTERY" (1891)

"I very clearly perceive that in your bedroom the window is upon the right-hand side, and yet I question whether Mr. Lestrade would have noted even so self-evident a thing as that."

"How on earth—!"

"My dear fellow, I know you well. I know the military neatness which characterizes you. You shave every morning, and in this season you shave by the sunlight, but since your shaving is less and less complete as we get farther back on the left side, until it becomes positively slovenly as we get round the angle of the jaw, it is surely very clear that that side is less illuminated than the other. I could not imagine a man of your habits looking at himself in an equal light and being satisfied with such a result. I only quote this as a trivial example of observation and inference."

AUGUST 7

THE VALLEY OF FEAR (1915)

"I am inclined to think—" said I.

"I should do so," Sherlock Holmes remarked impatiently.

I believe that I am one of the most long-suffering of mortals; but I'll admit that I was annoyed at the sardonic interruption. "Really, Holmes," said I severely, "you are a little trying at times."

AUGUST 8

A STUDY IN SCARLET (1887)

"It is a mistake to confound strangeness with mystery. The most commonplace crime is often the most mysterious, because it presents no new or special features from which deductions may be drawn. This murder would have been infinitely more difficult to unravel had the body of the victim been simply found lying in the roadway without any of those *outré* and sensational accompaniments which have rendered it remarkable. These strange details, far from making the case more difficult, have really had the effect of making it less so."

AUGUST 9

"THE ADVENTURE OF THE MAZARIN STONE" (1921)

Holmes looked at him thoughtfully like a master chess-player who meditates his crowning move. Then he threw open the table drawer and drew out a squat notebook.

"Do you know what I keep in this book?"

"No, sir, I do not!"

"You!"

"Me!"

"Yes, sir, *you*! You are all here—every action of your vile and dangerous life."

AUGUST 10

"You will not apply my precept," he said, shaking his head. "How often have I said to you that when you have eliminated the impossible, whatever remains, *however improbable*, must be the truth?"

AUGUST 11
"THE RED-HEADED LEAGUE" (1891)

"None the less you must come round to my view, for otherwise I shall keep piling fact upon fact on you, until your reason breaks down under them and acknowledges me to be right."

AUGUST 12
"A SCANDAL IN BOHEMIA" (1891)

"The facts are briefly these: Some five years ago, during a lengthy visit to Warsaw, I made the acquaintance of the well-known adventuress, Irene Adler. The name is no doubt familiar to you."

"Kindly look her up in my index, Doctor," murmured Holmes without opening his eyes. For many years he had adopted a system of docketing all paragraphs concerning men and things, so that it was difficult to name a subject or a person on which he could not at once furnish information. In this case I found her biography sandwiched in between that of a Hebrew Rabbi and that of a staff-commander who had written a monograph upon the deep-sea fishes.

AUGUST 13

THE SIGN OF FOUR (1890)

"I think you must recollect me, Mr. Athelney Jones," said Holmes quietly.

"Why, of course I do!" he wheezed. "It's Mr. Sherlock Holmes, the theorist. Remember you! I'll never forget how you lectured us all on causes and inferences and effects in the Bishopgate jewel case. It's true you set us on the right track; but you'll own now that it was more by good luck than good guidance."

"It was a piece of very simple reasoning."

"Oh, come, now, come! Never be ashamed to own up."

AUGUST 14

THE HOUND OF THE BASKERVILLES (1902)

"Footprints?"

"Footprints."

"A man's or a woman's?"

Dr. Mortimer looked strangely at us for an

instant, and his voice sank almost to a whisper as he answered:

"Mr. Holmes, they were the footprints of a gigantic hound!"

AUGUST 15

"THE FIVE ORANGE PIPS" (1891)

Sherlock Holmes sat for some time in silence, with his head sunk forward and his eyes bent upon the red glow of the fire. Then he lit his pipe, and leaning back in his chair he watched the blue smoke rings as they chased each other up to the ceiling.

"I think, Watson," he remarked at last, "that of all our cases we have had none more fantastic than this."

AUGUST 16

A STUDY IN SCARLET (1887)

"You have brought detection as near an exact science as it ever will be brought in this world."

My companion flushed up with pleasure at my words, and the earnest way in which I uttered them. I had already observed that he was as sensitive to flattery on the score of his art as any girl could be of her beauty.

"Indeed, I have found that it is usually in unimportant matters that there is a field for the observation, and for the quick analysis of cause and effect which gives the charm to an investigation. The larger crimes are apt to be the simpler, for the bigger the crime, the more obvious, as a rule, is the motive."

AUGUST 18
THE SIGN OF FOUR (1890)

"Very sorry, Mr. Thaddeus," said the porter inexorably. "Folk may be friends o' yours, and yet no friend o' the master's. He pays me well to do my duty, and my duty I'll do. I don't know none o' your friends."

"Oh, yes you do, McMurdo," cried Sherlock Holmes genially. "I don't think you can have forgotten me. Don't you remember that amateur who fought three rounds with you at Alison's rooms on the night of your benefit four years back?"

"Not Mr. Sherlock Holmes!" roared the prizefighter. "God's truth! how could I have mistook you? If instead o' standin' there so quiet you had just stepped up and given me that cross-hit of yours under the jaw, I'd ha' known you without a question. Ah, you're one that has wasted your gifts, you have! You might have aimed high, if you had joined the fancy."

"You see, Watson, if all else fails me, I have still one of the scientific professions open to me."

AUGUST 19

THE VALLEY OF FEAR (1915)

"The temptation to form premature theories upon insufficient data is the bane of our profession."

AUGUST 20

"THE RED-HEADED LEAGUE" (1891)

"As a rule," said Holmes, "the more bizarre a thing is the less mysterious it proves to be. It is your commonplace, featureless crimes which are really puzzling, just as a commonplace face is the most difficult to identify."

AUGUST 21

THE SIGN OF FOUR (1890)

"See here," said Holmes, pointing to the wooden hatchway. "We were hardly quick enough with our pistols." There, sure enough, just behind where we had been standing, stuck one of those murderous darts which we knew so well. It must have whizzed between us at the instant we fired. Holmes smiled at it and shrugged his shoulders in his easy fashion, but I confess that it turned me sick to think of the horrible death which had passed so close to us that night.

AUGUST 22

"THE DISAPPEARANCE OF
LADY FRANCES CARFAX" (1911)

"One of the most dangerous classes in the world," said he, "is the drifting and friendless woman. She is the most harmless and often the most useful of mortals, but she is the inevitable inciter of crime in others."

AUGUST 23

"THE GREEK INTERPRETER" (1893)

During my long and intimate acquaintance with Mr. Sherlock Holmes I had never heard him refer to his relations, and hardly ever to his own early life. This reticence upon his part had increased the somewhat inhuman effect which he produced upon me, until sometimes I found myself regarding him as an isolated phenomenon, a brain without a heart, as deficient in human sympathy as he was preeminent in intelligence. His aversion to women and his disinclination to form new friendships were both typical of his unemotional character, but not more so than his complete suppression of every reference to his own people. I had come to believe that he was an orphan with no relatives living; but one day, to my very great surprise, he began to talk to me about his brother.

AUGUST 24

"THE ADVENTURE OF THE
BRUCE-PARTINGTON PLANS" (1908)

"By the way, do you know what Mycroft is?"

I had some vague recollection of an explanation at the time of the Adventure of the Greek Interpreter.

"You told me that he had some small office under the British government."

Holmes chuckled.

"I did not know you quite so well in those days. One has to be discreet when one talks of high matters of state. You are right in thinking that he is under the British government. You would also be right in a sense if you said that occasionally he *is* the British government."

AUGUST 25

"THE GREEK INTERPRETER" (1893)

"If the art of the detective began and ended in reasoning from an armchair, my brother would be the greatest criminal agent that ever lived. But he has no ambition and no energy. He will not even go out of his way to verify his own solutions, and would rather be considered wrong than take the trouble to prove himself right."

AUGUST 26

"THE ADVENTURE OF THE
BRUCE-PARTINGTON PLANS" (1908)

"[Mycroft] has the tidiest and most orderly brain, with the greatest capacity for storing facts, of any man living. . . . All other men are specialists, but his specialism is omniscience."

AUGUST 27

"THE GREEK INTERPRETER" (1893)

Mycroft Holmes was a much larger and stouter man than Sherlock. His body was absolutely corpulent, but his face, though massive, had preserved something of the sharpness of expression which was so remarkable in that of his brother. His eyes, which were of a peculiarly light, watery grey, seemed to always retain that far-away, introspective look which I had only observed in Sherlock's when he was exerting his full powers.

"I am glad to meet you, sir," said he, putting out a broad, fat hand like the flipper of a seal. "I hear of Sherlock everywhere since you became his chronicler. By the way, Sherlock, I expected to see you round last week to consult me over that Manor House case. I thought you might be a little out of your depth."

"No, I solved it," said my friend, smiling.

"It was Adams, of course."

"Yes, it was Adams."

"I was sure of it from the first."

AUGUST 28

"THE ADVENTURE OF THE
BRUCE-PARTINGTON PLANS" (1908)

"It is as if you met a tram-car coming down a country lane. Mycroft has his rails and he runs on them. His Pall Mall lodgings, the Diogenes Club, Whitehall —that is his cycle. Once, and only once, he has been here. What upheaval can possibly have derailed him?"

AUGUST 29

"THE ADVENTURE OF THE
BRUCE-PARTINGTON PLANS" (1908)

"What is there for us to do?"

"To act, Sherlock—to act!" cried Mycroft, springing to his feet. "All my instincts are against this explanation. Use your powers! Go to the scene of the crime! See the people concerned! Leave no stone unturned! In all your career you have never had so great a chance of serving your country."

"Well, well!" said Holmes, shrugging his shoulders.

AUGUST 30

"We have him, Watson, we have him, and I dare swear that before to-morrow night he will be fluttering in our net as helpless as one of his own butterflies. A pin, a cork, and a card, and we add him to the Baker Street collection!" He burst into one of his rare fits of laughter as he turned away from the picture. I have not heard him laugh often, and it has always boded ill to somebody.

AUGUST 31

"Holmes," I said, "you have drawn a net round this man from which he cannot escape, and you have saved an innocent human life as truly as if you had cut the cord which was hanging him. I see the direction in which all this points. The culprit is—"

"Mr. John Turner," cried the hotel waiter, opening the door of our sitting-room, and ushering in a visitor.

SEPTEMBER

It was a September evening, and not yet seven o'clock, but the day had been a dreary one, and a dense drizzly fog lay low upon the great city. Mud-coloured clouds drooped sadly over the muddy streets. Down the Strand the lamps were but misty splotches of diffused light which threw a feeble circular glimmer upon the slimy pavement. The yellow glare from the shop-windows streamed out into the steamy, vaporous air and threw a murky, shifting radiance across the crowded thoroughfare. There was, to my mind, something eerie and ghost-like in the endless procession of faces which flitted across these narrow bars of light—sad faces and glad, haggard and merry. Like all humankind, they flitted from the gloom into the light, and so back into the gloom once more.

The Sign of Four (1890)

SEPTEMBER 1

"THE NAVAL TREATY" (1893)

"A very commonplace little murder," said he. "You've got something better, I fancy. You are the stormy petrel of crime, Watson."

SEPTEMBER 2

"THE 'GLORIA SCOTT'" (1893)

"You never heard me talk of Victor Trevor?" he asked. "He was the only friend I made during the two years I was at college. I was never a very sociable fellow, Watson, always rather fond of moping in my rooms and working out my own little methods of thought, so that I never mixed much with the men of my year. Bar fencing and boxing I had few athletic tastes, and then my line of study was quite distinct from that of the other fellows, so that we had no points of contact at all. Trevor was the only man I knew, and that only through the accident of his bull terrier freezing on to my ankle one morning as I went down to chapel.

"It was a prosaic way of forming a friendship, but it was effective."

"Strange," said I, "how terms of what in another man I should call laziness alternate with your fits of splendid energy and vigour."

"Yes," he answered, "there are in me the makings of a very fine loafer, and also of a pretty spry sort of a fellow."

"I think that you had better return to England, Watson."

"Why?"

"Because you will find me a dangerous companion now. This man's occupation is gone. He is lost if he returns to London. If I read his character right he will devote his whole energies to revenging himself upon me. He said as much in our short interview, and I fancy that he meant it. I should certainly recommend you to return to your practice."

It was hardly an appeal to be successful with one who was an old campaigner as well as an old friend.

SEPTEMBER 5

"Come, come, sir," said Holmes, laughing. "You are like my friend, Dr. Watson, who has a bad habit of telling his stories wrong end foremost."

SEPTEMBER 6

It was one Sunday evening early in September of the year 1903 that I received one of Holmes's laconic messages:

Come at once if convenient—if inconvenient come all the same.

SEPTEMBER 7

"Do you know, Watson," said Holmes, as we sat together in the gathering darkness, "I really have some scruples as to taking you to-night. There is a distinct element of danger."

"Can I be of assistance?"

"Your presence might be invaluable."

"Then I shall certainly come."

"It is very kind of you."

SEPTEMBER 8

"Look here, Watson; you look regularly done. Lie down there on the sofa and see if I can put you to sleep."

He took up his violin from the corner, and as I stretched myself out he began to play some low, dreamy, melodious air—his own, no doubt, for he had a remarkable gift for improvisation. I have a vague remembrance of his gaunt limbs, his earnest face and the rise and fall of his bow. Then I seemed to be floated peacefully away upon a soft sea of sound until I found myself in dreamland, with the sweet face of Mary Morstan looking down upon me.

SEPTEMBER 9

"THE ADVENTURE OF
THE SOLITARY CYCLIST" (1903)

"You really have done remarkably badly. He returns to the house, and you want to find out who he is. You come to a London house agent!"

"What should I have done?" I cried, with some heat.

"Gone to the nearest public-house. That is the centre of country gossip. They would have told you every name, from the master to the scullery-maid."

"To the man who loves art for its own sake," remarked Sherlock Holmes, tossing aside the advertisement sheet of the *Daily Telegraph*, "it is frequently in its least important and lowliest manifestations that the keenest pleasure is to be derived. It is pleasant to me to observe, Watson, that you have so far grasped this truth that in these little records of our cases which you have been good enough to draw up, and, I am bound to say, occasionally to embellish, you have given prominence not so much to the many *causes célèbres* and sensational trials in which I have figured but rather to those incidents which may have been trivial in themselves, but which have given room for those faculties of deduction and of logical synthesis which I have made my special province."

"I never guess. It is a shocking habit—destructive to the logical faculty."

He had gone out before breakfast, and I had sat down to mine when he strode into the room, his hat upon his head and a huge barbed-headed spear tucked like an umbrella under his arm.

"Good gracious, Holmes!" I cried. "You don't mean to say that you have been walking about London with that thing?"

"I drove to the butcher's and back."

"The butcher's?"

"And I return with an excellent appetite. There can be no question, my dear Watson, of the value of exercise before breakfast."

Sherlock Holmes was too irritable for conversation and too restless for sleep. I left him smoking hard, with his heavy, dark brows knotted together, and his long, nervous fingers tapping upon the arms of his chair, as he turned over in his mind every possible solution of the mystery.

SEPTEMBER 14

"It has been a duel between you and me, Mr. Holmes. You hope to place me in the dock. I tell you that I will never stand in the dock. You hope to beat me. I tell that you will never beat me. If you are clever enough to bring destruction upon me, rest assured that I shall do as much to you."

"You have paid me several compliments, Mr. Moriarty," said [Holmes]. "Let me pay you one in return when I say that if I were assured of the former eventuality I would, in the interests of the public, cheerfully accept the latter."

SEPTEMBER 15

"You have a theory then, [Inspector Baynes]?"

"And I'll work it myself, Mr. Holmes. It's only due to my own credit to do so. Your name is made, but I still have to make mine. I should be glad to be able to say afterwards that I had solved it without your help."

"Well, and there is the end of our little drama," I remarked, after we had sat some time smoking in silence. "I fear that it may be the last investigation in which I shall have the chance of studying your methods. Miss Morstan has done me the honour to accept me as a husband in prospective."

He gave a most dismal groan.

"I feared as much," said he. "I really cannot congratulate you."

I was a little hurt.

"Have you any reason to be dissatisfied with my choice?" I asked.

"Not at all. I think she is one of the most charming young ladies I ever met and might have been most useful in such work as we have been doing. She had a decided genius that way; witness the way in which she preserved that Agra plan from all the other papers of her father. But love is an emotional thing, and whatever is emotional is opposed to that true cold reason which I place above all things. I should never marry myself, lest I bias my judgment."

"I trust," said I, laughing, "that my judgment may survive the ordeal."

"Now, my dear Watson, is it beyond the limits of human ingenuity to furnish an explanation which would cover both these big facts? If it were one which would also admit of the mysterious note with its very curious phraseology, why, then it would be worth accepting as a temporary hypothesis. If the fresh facts which come to our knowledge all fit themselves into the scheme, then our hypothesis may gradually become a solution."

"But what is our hypothesis?"

Holmes leaned back in his chair with half-closed eyes.

"Well, what are we to do now?" asked MacDonald with some gruffness.

"Possess our souls in patience and make as little noise as possible," Holmes answered.

SEPTEMBER 19
"THE ADVENTURE OF THE COPPER BEECHES" (1892)

"I have frequently gained my first real insight into the character of parents by studying their children."

SEPTEMBER 20
"THE FIVE ORANGE PIPS" (1891)

"It was in January, '85, that my poor father met his end, and two years and eight months have elapsed since then. During that time I have lived happily at Horsham, and I had begun to hope that this curse had passed away from the family, and that it had ended with the last generation. I had begun to take comfort too soon, however; yesterday morning the blow fell in the very shape in which it had come upon my father."

SEPTEMBER 21
"THE ADVENTURE OF THE MAZARIN STONE" (1921)

The Count had risen from his chair, and his hand was behind his back. Holmes held something half protruding from the pocket of his dressing-gown.

"You won't die in your bed, Holmes."

"I have often had the same idea. Does it matter

very much? After all, Count, your own exit is more likely to be perpendicular than horizontal."

SEPTEMBER 22

"THE ADVENTURE OF CHARLES AUGUSTUS MILVERTON" (1904)

"You would not call me a marrying man, Watson?"

"No, indeed!"

"You'll be interested to hear that I'm engaged."

"My dear fellow! I congrat—"

"To Milverton's housemaid."

"Good heavens, Holmes!"

"I wanted information, Watson."

"Surely you have gone too far?"

"It was a most necessary step."

SEPTEMBER 23

THE SIGN OF FOUR (1890)

"It is of the first importance," he said, "not to allow your judgment to be biased by personal qualities. A client is to me a mere unit, a factor in a problem. The emotional qualities are antagonistic to clear reasoning. I assure you that the most winning woman I ever knew was hanged for poisoning three little children for their insurance-money, and the most repellent man of my acquaintance is a philanthropist who has spent nearly a quarter of a million upon the London poor."

SEPTEMBER 24

"THE RED-HEADED LEAGUE" (1891)

"What are you going to do, then?" I asked.

"To smoke," he answered. "It is quite a three pipe problem, and I beg that you won't speak to me for fifty minutes."

SEPTEMBER 25

"THE MAN WITH THE TWISTED LIP" (1891)

He took off his coat and waistcoat, put on a large blue dressing-gown, and then wandered about the room collecting pillows from his bed and cushions from the sofa and armchairs. With these he constructed a sort of Eastern divan, upon which he perched himself cross-legged, with an ounce of shag tobacco and a box of matches laid out in front of him.

SEPTEMBER 26

He sat coiled in his armchair, his haggard and ascetic face hardly visible amid the blue swirl of his tobacco smoke, his black brows drawn down, his forehead contracted, his eyes vacant and far away. Finally he laid down his pipe and sprang to his feet.

"It won't do, Watson!" said he with a laugh. "Let us walk along the cliffs together and search for flint arrows. We are more likely to find them than clues to this problem. To let the brain work without sufficient material is like racing an engine. It racks itself to pieces. The sea air, sunshine, and patience, Watson—all else will come."

SEPTEMBER 27

For a whole day my companion had rambled about the room with his chin upon his chest and his brows knitted, charging and recharging his pipe with the strongest black tobacco, and absolutely deaf to any of my questions or remarks. Fresh editions of every paper had been sent up by our news agent, only to be glanced over and tossed down into a corner. Yet, silent as he was, I knew perfectly well what it was over which he was brooding. There was but one problem before the public which could challenge his powers of analysis, and that was the singular disappearance of the favourite for the Wessex Cup, and the tragic murder of its trainer. When, therefore, he suddenly announced his intention of setting out for the scene of the drama, it was only what I had both expected and hoped for.

SEPTEMBER 28

"THE FIVE ORANGE PIPS" (1891)

It was in the latter days of September, and the equinoctial gales had set in with exceptional violence. All day the wind had screamed and the rain had beaten against the windows, so that even here in the heart of great, hand-made London we were forced to raise our minds for the instant from the routine of life, and to recognize the presence of those great elemental forces which shriek at mankind through the bars of his civilization, like untamed beasts in a cage. As evening drew in, the storm grew higher and louder, and the wind cried and sobbed like a child in the chimney. Sherlock Holmes sat moodily at one side of the fireplace cross-indexing his records of crime, whilst I at the other was deep in one of Clark Russell's fine sea-stories, until the howl of the gale from without seemed to blend with the text, and the splash of the rain to lengthen out into the long swash of the sea waves.

SEPTEMBER 29

Suddenly there broke from the silence of the night the most horrible cry to which I have ever listened. It swelled up louder and louder, a hoarse yell of pain and fear and anger all mingled in one dreadful shriek. They say that away down in the village, and even in the distant parsonage, that cry raised the sleepers from their beds. It struck cold to our hearts, and I stood gazing at Holmes, and he at me, until the last echoes of it had died away into the silence from which it rose.

"What can it mean?" I gasped.

"It means that it is all over," Holmes answered. "And perhaps, after all, it is for the best."

SEPTEMBER 30

I could not help laughing at the ease with which he explained his process of deduction. "When I hear you give your reasons," I remarked, "the thing always appears to me to be so ridiculously simple that I could easily do it myself, though at each successive instance of your reasoning I am baffled, until you explain your process."

OCTOBER

It was a wild morning in October, and I observed as I was dressing how the last remaining leaves were being whirled from the solitary plane tree which graces the yard behind our house. I descended to breakfast prepared to find my companion in depressed spirits, for, like all great artists, he was easily impressed by his surroundings. On the contrary, I found that he had nearly finished his meal, and that his mood was particularly bright and joyous, with that somewhat sinister cheerfulness which was characteristic of his lighter moments.

"You have a case, Holmes?" I remarked.

"The faculty of deduction is certainly contagious."

"The Problem of Thor Bridge" (1922)

OCTOBER 1

"You see," he said with a significant raising of the eyebrows.

In the light of the lantern I read with a thrill of horror, "The sign of the four."

"In God's name, what does it all mean?" I asked.

"It means murder."

OCTOBER 2

"And you, a trained man of science, believe it to be supernatural?"

"I do not know what to believe."

Holmes shrugged his shoulders.

"I have hitherto confined my investigations to this world," said he. "In a modest way I have combated evil, but to take on the Father of Evil himself would, perhaps, be too ambitious a task."

OCTOBER 3

"We are going well," said he, looking out of the window and glancing at his watch. "Our rate at present is fifty-three and a half miles an hour."

"I have not observed the quarter-mile posts," said I.

"Nor have I. But the telegraph posts upon this line are sixty yards apart, and the calculation is a simple one."

OCTOBER 4

THE HOUND OF THE BASKERVILLES (1902)

"You will see how impossible it is for me to go to Dartmoor."

"Whom would you recommend, then?"

Holmes laid his hand upon my arm.

"If my friend would undertake it there is no man who is better worth having at your side when you are in a tight place. No one can say so more confidently than I."

OCTOBER 5

"THE ADVENTURE OF CHARLES AUGUSTUS
MILVERTON" (1904)

Holmes had remarkable powers, carefully cultivated, of seeing in the dark.

OCTOBER 6

"You come at a crisis, Watson," said he. "If this paper remains blue, all is well. If it turns red, it means a man's life." He dipped it into the test-tube and it flushed at once into a dull, dirty crimson. "Hum! I thought as much!" he cried.

OCTOBER 7

"Holmes," I cried, "I seem to see dimly what you are hinting at. We are only just in time to prevent some subtle and horrible crime."

"Subtle enough, and horrible enough. When a doctor does go wrong, he is the first of criminals. He has nerve and he has knowledge."

OCTOBER 8

"It has been an intellectual treat to me to see the way in which you have grappled with this affair, and I say, unaffectedly, that it would be a grief to me to be forced to take any extreme measure. You smile, sir, but I assure you that it really would."

"Danger is part of my trade," [Holmes] remarked.

"This is not danger," said [Moriarty]. "It is inevitable destruction."

OCTOBER 9
"THE RED-HEADED LEAGUE" (1891)

"The door was shut and locked, with a little square of card-board hammered on to the middle of the panel with a tack. Here it is, and you can read for yourself."

He held up a piece of white card-board about the size of a sheet of note-paper. It read in this fashion—

THE RED-HEADED LEAGUE
IS
DISSOLVED.
October 9, 1890

OCTOBER 10
THE SIGN OF FOUR (1890)

My mind ran upon our late visitor—her smiles, the deep rich tones of her voice, the strange mystery which overhung her life. If she were seventeen at the time of her father's disappearance she must be seven-and-twenty now—a sweet age, when youth has lost its self-consciousness and become a little sobered by experience.

OCTOBER 11

"It has long been an axiom of mine that the little things are infinitely the most important."

OCTOBER 12

I had seen little of Holmes lately. My marriage had drifted us away from each other. My own complete happiness, and the home-centred interests which rise up around the man who first finds himself master of his own establishment, were sufficient to absorb all my attention; while Holmes, who loathed every form of society with his whole Bohemian soul, remained in our lodgings in Baker Street, buried among his old books, and alternating from week to week between cocaine and ambition, the drowsiness of the drug, and the fierce energy of his own keen nature. He was still, as ever, deeply attracted by the study of crime, and occupied his immense faculties and extraordinary powers of observation in following out those clues, and clearing up those mysteries which had been abandoned as hopeless by the official police.

OCTOBER 13

"That one word, my dear Watson, should have told me the whole story had I been the ideal reasoner which you are so fond of depicting."

OCTOBER 14

"THE MAN WITH THE TWISTED LIP" (1891)

Sherlock Holmes was a man, however, who, when he had an unsolved problem upon his mind, would go for days, and even for a week, without rest, turning it over, rearranging his facts, looking at it from every point of view, until he had either fathomed it, or convinced himself that his data were insufficient.

OCTOBER 15

"THE ADVENTURE OF THE CREEPING MAN" (1923)

It was a fine night, but chilly, and we were glad of our warm overcoats. There was a breeze, and clouds were scudding across the sky, obscuring from time to time the half-moon. It would have been a dismal vigil were it not for the expectation and excitement which carried us along, and the assurance of my comrade that we had probably reached the end of the strange sequence of events which had engaged our attention.

OCTOBER 16

"THE GREEK INTERPRETER" (1893)

"It will not be an easy door to force, but we will try if we cannot make someone hear us."

He hammered loudly at the knocker and pulled at the bell, but without any success. Holmes had slipped away, but he came back in a few minutes.

"I have a window open," said he.

"It is a mercy that you are on the side of the force, and not against it, Mr. Holmes," remarked the inspector as he noted the clever way in which my friend had forced back the catch.

OCTOBER 17

THE SIGN OF FOUR (1890)

"I never make exceptions. An exception disproves the rule."

OCTOBER 18

"But why not eat?"

"Because the faculties become refined when you starve them. Why, surely, as a doctor, my dear Watson, you must admit that what your digestion gains in the way of blood supply is so much lost to the brain. I am a brain, Watson. The rest of me is a mere appendix. Therefore, it is the brain I must consider."

OCTOBER 19

"That hurts my pride, Watson," he said at last. "It is a petty feeling, no doubt, but it hurts my pride. It becomes a personal matter with me now, and, if God sends me health, I shall set my hand upon this gang. That he should come to me for help, and that I should send him away to his death—!"

OCTOBER 20

Making our way among the trees, we reached the lawn, crossed it, and were about to enter through the window, when out from a clump of laurel bushes there darted what seemed to be a hideous and dis-torted child, who threw itself upon the grass with writhing limbs and then ran swiftly across the lawn into the darkness.

"My God!" I whispered; "did you see it?"

Holmes was for the moment as startled as I. His hand closed like a vise upon my wrist in his agita-tion. Then he broke into a low laugh and put his lips to my ear.

"It is a nice household," he murmured. "That is the baboon."

OCTOBER 21

"THE ADVENTURE OF THE COPPER BEECHES" (1892)

"But in avoiding the sensational, I fear that you may have bordered on the trivial."

"The end may have been so," I answered, "but the methods I hold to have been novel and of interest."

"Pshaw, my dear fellow, what do the public, the great unobservant public, who could hardly tell a weaver by his tooth or a compositor by his left thumb, care about the finer shades of analysis and deduction!"

OCTOBER 22

"One should always look for a possible alternative, and provide against it. It is the first rule of criminal investigation."

OCTOBER 23

THE SIGN OF FOUR (1890)

As we drove away I stole a glance back, and I still seem to see that little group on the step—the two graceful, clinging figures, the half-opened door, the hall-light shining through stained glass, the barometer, and the bright stair-rods. It was soothing to catch even that passing glimpse of a tranquil English home in the midst of the wild, dark business which had absorbed us.

OCTOBER 24

"A SCANDAL IN BOHEMIA" (1891)

He disappeared into his bedroom, and returned in a few minutes in the character of an amiable and simple-minded Nonconformist clergyman. His broad black hat, his baggy trousers, his white tie, his sympathetic smile, and general look of peering and benevolent curiosity were such as Mr. John Hare alone could have equalled. It was not merely that

Holmes changed his costume. His expression, his manner, his very soul seemed to vary with every fresh part that he assumed. The stage lost a fine actor, even as science lost an acute reasoner, when he became a specialist in crime.

OCTOBER 25

"THE MAN WITH THE TWISTED LIP" (1891)

As I passed the tall man who sat by the brazier I felt a sudden pluck at my skirt, and a low voice whispered, "Walk past me, and then look back at me." The words fell quite distinctly upon my ear. I glanced down. They could only have come from the old man at my side, and yet he sat now as absorbed as ever, very thin, very wrinkled, bent with age, an opium pipe dangling down from between his knees, as though it had dropped in sheer lassitude from his fingers. I took two steps forward and looked back. It took all my self-control to prevent me from breaking out into a cry of astonishment. He had turned his back so that none could see him but I. His form had filled out, his wrinkles were gone, the dull eyes had regained their fire, and there, sitting by the fire and grinning at my surprise, was none other than Sherlock Holmes.

OCTOBER 26

"A SCANDAL IN BOHEMIA" (1891)

"I left the house a little after eight o'clock this morning in the character of a groom out of work. There is a wonderful sympathy and freemasonry among horsy men. Be one of them, and you will know all that there is to know."

OCTOBER 27

"THE ADVENTURE OF CHARLES AUGUSTUS MILVERTON" (1904)

Holmes sat motionless by the fire, his hands buried deep in his trouser pockets, his chin sunk upon his breast, his eyes fixed upon the glowing embers. For half an hour he was silent and still. Then, with the gesture of a man who has taken his decision, he sprang to his feet and passed into his bedroom. A little later a rakish young workman, with a goatee beard and a swagger, lit his clay pipe at the lamp before descending into the street. "I'll be back some time, Watson," said he, and vanished into the night.

OCTOBER 28

"A SCANDAL IN BOHEMIA" (1891)

It was close upon four before the door opened, and a drunken-looking groom, ill-kempt and side-whiskered, with an inflamed face and disreputable clothes, walked into the room. Accustomed as I was to my friend's amazing powers in the use of disguises, I had to look three times before I was certain that it was indeed he.

OCTOBER 29

THE SIGN OF FOUR (1890)

"I think that you might offer me a cigar too," he said.

We both started in our chairs. There was Holmes sitting close to us with an air of quiet amusement.

"Holmes!" I exclaimed. "You here! But where is the old man?"

"Here is the old man," said he, holding out a heap of white hair. "Here he is—wig, whiskers, eyebrows, and all. I thought my disguise was pretty good, but I hardly expected that it would stand that test."

OCTOBER 30

"THE MAN WITH THE TWISTED LIP" (1891)

Holmes stooped to the water jug, moistened his sponge, and then rubbed it twice vigorously across and down the prisoner's face.

"Let me introduce you," he shouted, "to Mr. Neville St. Clair, of Lee, in the county of Kent."

Never in my life have I seen such a sight. The man's face peeled off under the sponge like the bark from a tree. Gone was the coarse brown tint! Gone, too, was the horrid scar which had seamed it across, and the twisted lip which had given the repulsive sneer to the face! A twitch brought away the tangled red hair, and there, sitting up in his bed, was a pale, sad-faced, refined-looking man, black-haired and smooth-skinned, rubbing his eyes and staring about him with sleepy bewilderment.

OCTOBER 31

THE HOUND OF THE BASKERVILLES (1902)

A hound it was, an enormous coal-black hound, but not such a hound as mortal eyes have ever seen. Fire burst from its open mouth, its eyes glowed with a smouldering glare, its muzzle and hackles and dewlap were outlined in flickering flame. Never in the delirious dream of a disordered brain could anything more savage, more appalling, more hellish be conceived than that dark form and savage face which broke upon us out of the wall of fog.

NOVEMBER

"It was a wild night. The wind was howling outside, and the rain was beating and splashing against the windows. Suddenly, amidst all of the hubbub of the gale, there burst forth the wild scream of a terrified woman."—*Helen Stoner*

"The Adventure of the Speckled Band" (1892)

NOVEMBER 1

"Do not think of revenge, or anything of the sort, at present. I think that we may gain that by means of the law; but we have our web to weave, while theirs is already woven."

NOVEMBER 2

"You are sure that she has not sent it yet?"

"I am sure."

"And why?"

"Because she has said that she would send it on the day when the betrothal was publicly proclaimed. That will be next Monday."

"Oh, then we have three days yet," said Holmes, with a yawn.

NOVEMBER 3

"Run down, my dear fellow, and open the door, for all virtuous folk have been long in bed."

NOVEMBER 4

"Circumstantial evidence is a very tricky thing," answered Holmes, thoughtfully. "It may seem to point very straight to one thing, but if you shift your own point of view a little, you may find it pointing in an equally uncompromising manner to something entirely different."

NOVEMBER 5

"Recognizing, as I do, that you are the second highest expert in Europe—"

"Indeed, sir! May I inquire who has the honour to be the first?" asked Holmes with some asperity.

"To the man of precisely scientific mind the work of Monsieur Bertillon must always appeal strongly."

"Then had you not better consult him?"

"I said, sir, to the precisely scientific mind. But as a practical man of affairs it is acknowledged that you stand alone. I trust, sir, that I have not inadvertently—"

"Just a little," said Holmes.

NOVEMBER 6

"THE ADVENTURE OF THE SIX NAPOLEONS" (1904)

"The affair seems absurdly trifling, and yet I dare call nothing trivial when I reflect that some of my most classic cases have had the least promising commencement. You will remember, Watson, how the dreadful business of the Abernetty family was first brought to my notice by the depth which the parsley had sunk into the butter upon a hot day."

NOVEMBER 7

"THE RED-HEADED LEAGUE" (1891)

"As a rule, when I have heard some slight indication of the course of events, I am able to guide myself by the thousands of other similar cases which occur to my memory. In the present instance I am forced to admit that the facts are, to the best of my belief, unique."

NOVEMBER 8

"THE ADVENTURE OF THE EMPTY HOUSE" (1903)

It was indeed like old times when, at that hour, I found myself seated beside him in a hansom, my revolver in my pocket, and the thrill of adventure in my heart. Holmes was cold and stern and silent. As the gleam of the street-lamps flashed upon his austere features, I saw that his brows were drawn down in thought and his thin lips compressed. I knew not what wild beast we were about to hunt down in the dark jungle of criminal London, but I was well assured, from the bearing of this master huntsman, that the adventure was a most grave one—while the sardonic smile which occasionally broke through his ascetic gloom boded little good for the object of our quest.

NOVEMBER 9

"A SCANDAL IN BOHEMIA" (1891)

"Wedlock suits you," he remarked, "I think, Watson, that you have put on seven and a half pounds since I saw you."

"Seven!" I answered.

"Indeed, I should have thought a little more. Just a trifle more, I fancy, Watson."

NOVEMBER 10

"THE ADVENTURE OF THE NOBLE BACHELOR" (1892)

"Draw your chair up, and hand me my violin, for the only problem we have still to solve is how to while away these bleak autumnal evenings."

"The Press, Watson, is a most valuable institution, if you only know how to use it."

Holmes's quiet day in the country had a singular termination, for he arrived at Baker Street late in the evening, with a cut lip and a discoloured lump upon his forehead, besides a general air of dissipation which would have made his own person the fitting object of a Scotland Yard investigation. He was immensely tickled by his own adventures and laughed heartily as he recounted them.

"I get so little active exercise that it is always a treat," said he. "You are aware that I have some proficiency in the good old British sport of boxing. Occasionally, it is of service; to-day, for example, I should have come to very ignominious grief without it."

NOVEMBER 13

"THE ADVENTURE OF THE DEVIL'S FOOT" (1910)

Holmes paced with light, swift steps about the room; he sat in the various chairs, drawing them up and reconstructing their positions. He tested how much of the garden was visible; he examined the floor, the ceiling, and the fireplace; but never once did I see that sudden brightening of his eyes and tightening of his lips which would have told me that he saw some gleam of light in this utter darkness.

NOVEMBER 14

THE SIGN OF FOUR (1890)

"The main thing with people of that sort," said Holmes as we sat in the sheets of the wherry, "is never to let them think that their information can be of the slightest importance to you. If you do they will instantly shut up like an oyster. If you listen to them under protest, as it were, you are very likely to get what you want."

NOVEMBER 15

"THE BOSCOMBE VALLEY MYSTERY" (1891)

"It was a confession," I ejaculated.

"No, for it was followed by a protestation of inno-cence."

"Coming on the top of such a damning series of events, it was at least a most suspicious remark."

"On the contrary," said Holmes, "it is the bright-est rift which I can at present see in the clouds."

NOVEMBER 16

"THE ADVENTURE OF THE BRUCE-PARTINGTON PLANS" (1908)

All the long November evening I waited, filled with impatience for his return. At last, shortly after nine o'clock, there arrived a messenger with a note:

Am dining at Goldini's Restaurant, Gloucester Road, Kensington. Please come at once and join me there. Bring with you a jemmy, a dark lantern, a chisel, and a revolver. —S. H.

NOVEMBER 17

"THE ADVENTURE OF THE PRIORY SCHOOL" (1904)

"I must take the view, your Grace, that when a man embarks upon a crime, he is morally guilty of any other crime which may spring from it."

NOVEMBER 18

"SILVER BLAZE" (1892)

"One true inference invariably suggests others."

NOVEMBER 19

"THE ADVENTURE OF THE BRUCE-PARTINGTON PLANS" (1908)

In the third week of November, in the year 1895, a dense yellow fog settled down upon London. From the Monday to the Thursday I doubt whether it was ever possible from our windows in Baker Street to see the loom of the opposite houses. The first day Holmes had spent in cross-indexing his huge book of references. The second and third had been patiently occupied upon a subject which he had recently made his hobby—the music of the Middle Ages. But when, for the fourth time, after pushing back our chairs from breakfast we saw the greasy, heavy brown swirl still drifting past us and condensing in oily drops upon the window-panes, my comrade's impatient and active nature could endure this drab existence no longer. He paced restlessly about our sitting-room in a fever of suppressed energy, biting his nails, tapping the furniture, and chafing against inaction.

"As you are aware, Watson, there is no one who knows the higher criminal world of London so well as I do. For years past I have continually been conscious of some power behind the malefactor, some deep organizing power which forever stands in the way of the law, and throws its shield over the wrong-doer. Again and again in cases of the most varying sorts—forgery cases, robberies, murders—I have felt the presence of this force, and I have deduced its action in many of those undiscovered crimes in which I have not been personally consulted. For years I have endeavoured to break through the veil which shrouded it, and at last the time came when I seized my thread and followed it, until it led me, after a thousand cunning windings, to ex-Professor Moriarty, of mathematical celebrity."

"You have probably never heard of Professor Moriarty?" said he.

"Never."

"Ay, there's the genius and the wonder of the thing!" he cried. "The man pervades London, and no one has heard of him. That's what puts him on a pinnacle in the records of crime. I tell you, Watson, in all seriousness, that if I could beat that man, if I could free society of him, I should feel that my own career had reached its summit, and I should be prepared to turn to some more placid line in life."

NOVEMBER 22

THE VALLEY OF FEAR (1915)

"I thought you told me once, Mr. Holmes, that you had never met Professor Moriarty," [asked Inspector MacDonald.]

"No, I never have."

"Then how do you know about his rooms?"

"Ah, that's another matter. I have been three times in his rooms, twice waiting for him under different pretexts and leaving before he came. Once— well, I can hardly tell about the once to an official detective."

NOVEMBER 23

"THE FINAL PROBLEM" (1893)

"I was sitting in my room thinking the matter over when the door opened and Professor Moriarty stood before me.

"My nerves are fairly proof, Watson, but I must confess to a start when I saw the very man who had been so much in my thoughts standing there on my threshold. His appearance was quite familiar to me. He is extremely tall and thin, his forehead domes out in a white curve, and his two eyes are deeply sunken in his head. He is clean-shaven, pale, and ascetic-looking, retaining something of the professor in his features. His shoulders are rounded from much study, and his face protrudes forward and is forever slowly oscillating from side to side in a curiously reptilian fashion."

NOVEMBER 24

"THE FINAL PROBLEM" (1893)

"You know my powers, my dear Watson, and yet at the end of three months I was forced to confess that I had at last met an antagonist who was my intellectual equal. My horror at his crimes was lost in my admiration at his skill."

NOVEMBER 25

"THE ADVENTURE OF THE NORWOOD BUILDER" (1903)

"From the point of view of the criminal expert," said Mr. Sherlock Holmes, "London has become a singularly uninteresting city since the death of the late lamented Professor Moriarty."

"I can hardly think that you would find many decent citizens to agree with you," I answered.

"Well, well, I must not be selfish."

NOVEMBER 26

"SILVER BLAZE" (1892)

"See the value of imagination," said Holmes. "It is the one quality which [Inspector] Gregory lacks. We imagined what might have happened, acted upon the supposition, and find ourselves justified. Let us proceed."

NOVEMBER 27

"THE ADVENTURE OF WISTERIA LODGE" (1908)

The whole inexplicable tangle seemed to straighten out before me. I wondered, as I always did, how it had not been obvious to me before.

NOVEMBER 28

"THE ADVENTURE OF THE GOLDEN PINCE-NEZ" (1904)

It was a wild, tempestuous night, towards the close of November. Holmes and I sat together in silence all the evening, he engaged with a powerful lens deciphering the remains of the original inscription upon a palimpsest, I deep in a recent treatise upon surgery. Outside the wind howled down Baker Street, while the rain beat fiercely against the windows. It was strange there, in the very depths of the town, with ten miles of man's handiwork on every side of us, to feel the iron grip of Nature, and to be conscious that to the huge elemental forces all London was no more than the molehills that dot the fields.

NOVEMBER 29

"THE ADVENTURE OF THE SPECKLED BAND" (1892)

Round his brow he had a peculiar yellow band, with brownish speckles, which seemed to be bound tightly round his head. As we entered he made neither sound nor motion.

"The band! the speckled band!" whispered Holmes.

I took a step forward. In an instant his strange headgear began to move, and there reared itself from among his hair the squat diamond-shaped head and puffed neck of a loathsome serpent.

"It is a swamp adder!" cried Holmes; "the deadliest snake in India. He has died within ten seconds of being bitten. Violence does, in truth, recoil upon the violent, and the schemer falls into the pit which he digs for another."

"My dear Holmes," said I, "this is too much. You would certainly have been burned, had you lived a few centuries ago."

DECEMBER

It was a bitter night, so we drew on our ulsters and wrapped cravats about our throats. Outside, the stars were shining coldly in a cloudless sky, and the breath of the passers-by blew out into smoke like so many pistol shots.

"The Adventure of the Blue Carbuncle" (1892)

DECEMBER 1

It was pleasant to Dr. Watson to find himself once more in the untidy room of the first floor in Baker Street which had been the starting-point of so many remarkable adventures. He looked round him at the scientific charts upon the wall, the acid-charred bench of chemicals, the violin-case leaning in the corner, the coal-scuttle, which contained of old the pipes and tobacco.

DECEMBER 2

"THE NAVAL TREATY" (1893)

"The most difficult crime to track is the one which is purposeless."

DECEMBER 3

"THE ADVENTURE OF WISTERIA LODGE" (1908)

It was not, I must confess, a very alluring prospect. The old house with its atmosphere of murder, the singular and formidable inhabitants, the unknown dangers of the approach, and the fact that we were putting ourselves legally in a false position all combined to damp my ardour. But there was something in the ice-cold reasoning of Holmes which made it impossible to shrink from any adventure which he might recommend. One knew that thus, and only thus, could a solution be found. I clasped his hand in silence, and the die was cast.

DECEMBER 4
"THE ADVENTURE OF THE MAZARIN STONE" (1921)

The prize-fighter, a heavily built young man with a stupid, obstinate, slab-sided face, stood awkwardly at the door, looking about him with a puzzled expression. Holmes's debonair manner was a new experience, and though he vaguely felt that it was hostile, he did not know how to counter it.

DECEMBER 5
"THE ADVENTURE OF CHARLES AUGUSTUS MILVERTON" (1904)

"You know, Watson, I don't mind confessing to you that I have always had an idea that I would have made a highly efficient criminal."

DECEMBER 6

"Once or twice in my career I feel that I have done more real harm by my discovery of the criminal than ever he had done by his crime. I have learned caution now, and I had rather play tricks with the law of England than with my own conscience."

DECEMBER 7

The day was just breaking when I woke to find the long, thin form of Holmes by my bedside. He was fully dressed, and had apparently already been out.

"I have done the lawn and the bicycle shed," said he. "I have also had a ramble through the Ragged Shaw. Now, Watson, there is cocoa ready in the next room. I must beg you to hurry, for we have a great day before us."

DECEMBER 8

"But I am prepared to bet that you will not guess the form that my exercise has taken."

"I will not attempt it."

He chuckled as he poured out the coffee.

"If you could have looked into Allardyce's back shop, you would have seen a dead pig swung from a hook in the ceiling, and a gentleman in his shirt sleeves furiously stabbing at it with this weapon. I was that energetic person, and I have satisfied myself that by no exertion of my strength can I transfix the pig with a single blow. Perhaps you would care to try?"

"Not for worlds."

DECEMBER 9

THE VALLEY OF FEAR (1915)

"Porlock is important, not for himself, but for the great man with whom he is in touch. Picture to yourself the pilot fish with the shark, the jackal with the lion—anything that is insignificant in companionship with what is formidable: not only formidable, Watson, but sinister—in the highest degree sinister. That is where he comes within my purview. You have heard me speak of Professor Moriarty?"

"The famous scientific criminal, as famous among crooks as—"

"My blushes, Watson!" Holmes murmured in a deprecating voice.

"I was about to say, as he is unknown to the public."

"A touch! A distinct touch!" cried Holmes. "You are developing a certain unexpected vein of pawky humour, Watson, against which I must learn to guard myself."

DECEMBER 10

"But what were his relations with the governess, and how did you discover them?"

"Bluff, Watson, bluff!"

DECEMBER 11

"There are no better instruments than discharged servants with a grievance, and I was lucky enough to find one."

DECEMBER 12

"I have heard your name, Mr. Sherlock Holmes, and I am aware of your profession—one of which I by no means approve."

"In that, Doctor [Armstrong], you will find yourself in agreement with every criminal in the country."

DECEMBER 13

"I have not all my facts yet, but I do not think there are any insuperable difficulties. Still, it is an error to argue in front of your data. You will find yourself insensibly twisting them round to fit your theories."

DECEMBER 14

"But you had retired, Holmes. We heard of you as living the life of a hermit among your bees and your books in a small farm upon the South Downs."

"Exactly, Watson. Here is a fruit of my leisured ease, the *magnum opus* of my latter years!" He picked up the volume from the table and read out the whole title, *Practical Handbook of Bee Culture, with Some Observations upon the Segregation of the Queen.* "Alone I did it. Behold the fruit of pensive nights and laborious days when I watched the little working gangs as once I watched the criminal world of London."

DECEMBER 15

THE VALLEY OF FEAR (1915)

"I said that I would play the game fairly by you, and I do not think it is a fair game to allow you for one unnecessary moment to waste your energies upon a profitless task. Therefore I am here to advise you this morning, and my advice to you is summed up in three words—abandon the case."

MacDonald and White Mason stared in amazement at their celebrated colleague.

"You consider it hopeless!" cried the inspector.

"I consider your case to be hopeless. I do not consider that it is hopeless to arrive at the truth."

DECEMBER 16

"THE ADVENTURE OF THE RED CIRCLE" (1911)

"Why should you go further in it? What have you to gain from it?"

"What, indeed? It is art for art's sake, Watson. I suppose when you doctored you found yourself studying cases without thought of a fee?"

"For my education, Holmes."

"Education never ends, Watson. It is a series of lessons with the greatest for the last. This is an instructive case. There is neither money nor credit in it, and yet one would wish to tidy it up."

DECEMBER 17

"The pressure of public opinion can do in the town what the law cannot accomplish. There is no lane so vile that the scream of a tortured child, or the thud of a drunkard's blow, does not beget sympathy and indignation among the neighbours, and then the whole machinery of justice is ever so close that a word of complaint can set it going, and there is but a step between the crime and the dock."

DECEMBER 18

A STUDY IN SCARLET (1887)

"I consider that a man's brain originally is like a little empty attic, and you have to stock it with such furniture as you choose. A fool takes in all the lumber of every sort that he comes across, so that the knowledge which might be useful to him gets crowded out, or at best is jumbled up with a lot of other things so that he has a difficulty in laying his hands upon it. Now the skilful workman is very careful indeed as to what he takes into his brain-attic. He will have nothing but the tools which may help him in doing his work, but of these he has a large assortment, and all in the most perfect order. It is a mistake to think that that little room has elastic walls and can distend to any extent. Depend upon it, there comes a time when for every addition of knowledge you forget something that you knew before. It is of the highest importance, therefore, not to have useless facts elbowing out the useful ones."

DECEMBER 19
"THE RESIDENT PATIENT" (1893)

"However, wretch as he was, he was still living under the shield of British law, and I have no doubt, Inspector, that you will see that, though the shield may fail to guard, the sword of justice is still there to avenge."

DECEMBER 20
"THE FINAL PROBLEM" (1893)

"I think that I may go so far as to say, Watson, that I have not lived wholly in vain," he remarked. "If my record were closed to-night I could still survey it with equanimity. The air of London is the sweeter for my presence. In over a thousand cases I am not aware that I have ever used my powers upon the wrong side. Of late I have been tempted to look into the problems furnished by nature rather than those more superficial ones for which our own artificial state of society is responsible. Your memoirs will draw to an end, Watson, upon the day that I crown my career by the capture or extinction of the most dangerous and capable criminal in Europe."

DECEMBER 21

"THE ADVENTURE OF WISTERIA LODGE" (1908)

I could tell by numerous subtle signs, which might have been lost upon anyone but myself, that Holmes was on a hot scent. As impassive as ever to the casual observer, there were none the less a subdued eagerness and suggestion of tension in his brightened eyes and brisker manner which assured me that the game was afoot.

DECEMBER 22

THE VALLEY OF FEAR (1915)

"I have worked with Mr. Holmes before," said Inspector MacDonald. "He plays the game."

"My own idea of the game, at any rate," said Holmes, with a smile. "I go into a case to help the ends of justice and the work of the police. If I have ever separated myself from the official force, it is because they have first separated themselves from me. I have no wish ever to score at their expense. At the same time, Mr. White Mason, I claim the right to work in my own way and give my results at my own time—complete rather than in stages."

DECEMBER 23

"THE ADVENTURE OF THE
BRUCE-PARTINGTON PLANS" (1908)

"Why do you not solve it yourself, Mycroft? You can see as far as I."

"Possibly, Sherlock. But it is a question of getting details. Give me your details, and from an armchair I will return you an excellent expert opinion. But to run here and run there, to cross-question railway guards, and lie on my face with a lens to my eye—it is not my *métier*. No, you are the one man who can clear the matter up. If you have a fancy to see your name in the next honours list—"

My friend smiled and shook his head.

"I play the game for the game's own sake," said he.

DECEMBER 24

"THE ADVENTURE OF THE MAZARIN STONE" (1921)

"Look here, Holmes, this is simply impossible. This is a desperate man, who sticks at nothing. He may have come to murder you."

"I should not be surprised."

"I insist upon staying with you."

"You would be horribly in the way."

"In *his* way?"

"No, my dear fellow—in my way."

"Well, I can't possibly leave you."

"Yes, you can, Watson. And you will, for you have never failed to play the game. I am sure you will play it to the end."

"I suppose that I am commuting a felony, but it is just possible that I am saving a soul. This fellow will not go wrong again. He is too terribly frightened. Send him to gaol now, and you make him a gaol-bird for life. Besides, it is the season of forgiveness. Chance has put in our way a most singular and whimsical problem, and its solution is its own reward. If you will have the goodness to touch the bell, Doctor, we will begin another investigation, in which also a bird will be the chief feature."

"There is nothing in which deduction is so necessary as in religion," said he, leaning with his back against the shutters. "It can be built up as an exact science by the reasoner. Our highest assurance of the goodness of Providence seems to me to rest in the flowers. All other things, our powers, our desires, our food, are all really necessary for our existence in the first instance. But this rose is an extra. Its smell and its colour are an embellishment of life, not a condition of it. It is only goodness which gives extras, and so I say again that we have much to hope from the flowers."

DECEMBER 27

"THE ADVENTURE OF THE BLUE CARBUNCLE" (1892)

I had called upon my friend Sherlock Holmes upon the second morning after Christmas, with the intention of wishing him the compliments of the season. He was lounging upon the sofa in a purple dressing-gown, a pipe-rack within his reach upon the right, and a pile of crumpled morning papers, evidently newly studied, near at hand. Beside the couch was a wooden chair, and on the angle of the back hung a very seedy and disreputable hard felt hat, much the worse for wear, and cracked in several places. A lens and a forceps lying upon the seat of the chair suggested that the hat had been suspended in this manner for the purpose of examination.

"You are engaged," said I; "perhaps I interrupt you."

"Not at all. I am glad to have a friend with whom I can discuss my results."

"Now, Watson, confess yourself utterly taken aback," said he.

"I am."

"I ought to make you sign a paper to that effect."

"Why?"

"Because in five minutes you will say that it is all so absurdly simple."

"I shall have him, Doctor—I'll lay you two to one that I have him. I must thank you for it all. I might not have gone but for you, and so have missed the finest study I ever came across: a study in scarlet, eh? Why shouldn't we use a little art jargon. There's the scarlet thread of murder running through the colourless skein of life, and our duty is to unravel it, and isolate it, and expose every inch of it."

"But what I can't make head or tail of, Mr. Holmes, is how on earth *you* got yourself mixed up in the matter."

"Education, Gregson, education. Still seeking knowledge at the old university. Well, Watson, you have one more specimen of the tragic and grotesque to add to your collection. By the way, it is not eight o'clock, and a Wagner night at Covent Garden! If we hurry, we might be in time for the second act."

"There's coffee on the table, Watson, and I have a cab at the door."

Index of Sources

To compile these quotations, we drew on a number of editions of Holmes stories, including the three wonderfully illustrated volumes of *The New Annotated Sherlock Holmes*, edited by Leslie S. Klinger (New York: W. W. Norton & Company, 2005–6), the compact and authoritative Oxford World's Classics editions, and, thanks to Google Books (friend to all contemporary literary detectives), a number of collections of the issues of the *Strand* in which the stories were first published.

"The Adventure of the Dancing Men," January 9, January 27, March 25, December 28

"The Adventure of the Devil's Foot," January 14, February 18, February 22, March 14, March 16, June 1, September 26, November 13

"The Adventure of the Dying Detective," January 30, February 26, April 11, April 27, June 13

"The Adventure of the Empty House," February 8, March 19, April 29, May 5, June 5, July 21, November 8

"The Adventure of the Engineer's Thumb," June 22

"The Adventure of the Golden Pince-Nez," January 5, November 3, November 28

"The Adventure of the Mazarin Stone," March 29, April 7, June 12, August 9, September 21, October 18, December 1, December 4, December 24

"The Adventure of the Missing Three-Quarter," February 19, February 21, March 21, May 23, July 13, December 12

"The Adventure of the Noble Bachelor," June 6, November 10

"The Adventure of the Norwood Builder," April 17, June 29, November 25

"The Adventure of the Priory School," March 26, November 17, December 7

"The Adventure of the Red Circle," February (general), February 17, March 15, March 18, April 20, May 8, June 10, December 16, December 30

"The Adventure of the Second Stain," March 28, April 19, May 31, June 18

"The Adventure of the Six Napoleons," February 7, February 28, June 27, June 30, November 6, November 11, December 31

"The Adventure of the Solitary Cyclist," May (general), September 9, November 12

"The Adventure of the Speckled Band," March 1, March 7, April 3, April 8, May 2, May 18, May 26, June 2, June 8, July 16, July 20, July 24, August 4, September 7, September 29,

October 7, October 20, November (general), November 29

"The Adventure of the Three Students," February 2

"The Adventure of Wisteria Lodge," March (general), March 27, August 1, September 5, September 15, September 17, November 27, December 3, December 11, December 13, December 21

"The Boscombe Valley Mystery," January 25, February 10, March 11, March 17, March 24, June 3, June 25, July 5, July 12, August 6, August 31, November 4, November 15

"The Cardboard Box," April 25, April 28, August (general)

"A Case of Identity," January 26, February 1, March 3, March 10, May 1, May 11, June 4, August 17, October 11

"The Crooked Man," October 13

"The Disappearance of Lady Frances Carfax," January 10, February 9, March 13, May 14, July 18, August 22, September 13

The Extraordinary Adventures of Arsène Lupin, Gentleman-Burglar (by Maurice Leblanc, translated by George Morehead), February 29

"The Final Problem," April 24, May 3, May 4, July 29, September 4, September 14, October 8, November 20, November 21, November 23, November 24, December 20

"The Five Orange Pips," January 4, January 12, February 3, February 11, March 30, April 2, July 31, August 15, September 20, September 28, October 19, November 1

"The Giant Rat of Sumatra," referenced as the source for our April 1 quote, is a case mentioned in "The Adventure of the Sussex Vampire," but the story of that case was never published. The origin of this familiar noncanonical line is disputed.

"The 'Gloria Scott,'" September 2

"The Greek Interpreter," January 11, March 12, July 10, August 23, August 25, August 27, October 16

"His Last Bow," August 2, December 14

The Hound of the Baskervilles, January 19, April 15, April 21,